D0812025

KEVIN BALDEOSINGH was educated at the University of the West Indies, and also got a degree there. After teaching for three years, he was hired by Owen Baptiste, then editor-in-chief of Trinidad Express Newspapers, as an editorial writer and columnist.

After three years at the *Express*, he moved across to the country's other daily newspaper, the Trinidad *Guardian*, where he currently works as an assistant editor.

He likes squash, volleyball, tennis and the women who play them. Born in 1963, he is still young, and single, but hopes to get older one day.

KEVIN BALDEOSINGH

THE AUTOBIOGRAPHY
OF
PARAS P.

Heinemann

Heinemann Educational Publishers
A Division of Heinemann Publishers (Oxford) Ltd
Halley Court, Jordan Hill, Oxford OX2 8EJ

Heinemann: A Division of Reed Publishing (USA) Inc.
361 Hanover Street, Portsmouth, NH 03801–3912, USA

Heinemann Educational Books (Nigeria) Ltd
PMB 5205, Ibadan

Heinemann Educational Botswana Publishers (Pty) Ltd
PO Box 10103, Village Post Office, Gaborone, Botswana

FLORENCE   PRAGUE   PARIS   MADRID
ATHENS   MELBOURNE   JOHANNESBURG
AUCKLAND   SINGAPORE   TOKYO
CHICAGO   SAO PAULO

First published by Heinemann Educational Publishers 1996

British Library Cataloguing in Publication Data
A catalogue record for this book is available from the British Library.

ISBN 0 435 988182

Edited by Katharina Hamza
Cover design by Touchpaper
Cover illustration by Spike Gerrell
Author photograph by Sean Drakes

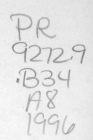
Photoset by CentraCet Limited, Cambridge
Printed and bound in Great Britain by
Cox & Wyman Ltd, Reading, Berkshire

96 97 98 99 8 7 6 5 4 3 2 1

For my mother and my father, who should not be held responsible for opinions expressed in this book.

Methinks my life is a twice-written scroll
Scrawled over on some boyish holiday
With idle songs for pipe and virelay,
Which do but mar the secret of the whole.

From 'Hélas' by Oscar Wilde

Editor's Note

About one year before his death, Mr Paras Parmanandansingh contacted me with a request that I edit his autobiography. However, the project was shelved when he learned he had to pay for such services.

But, after two months, he changed his mind and we agreed upon a fee. He then informed me that I was not to alter, prune or rewrite his manuscript in any way. He wanted me only to correct his spelling and grammar. He explained that he was an excellent writer, but had always had trouble in those two areas. He also wanted me to find appropriate quotes for each chapter of his autobiography since he was too busy to do so himself.

Nonetheless, I did persuade Mr Parmanandansingh to reduce the size of his manuscript. He had been working on it for the past ten years, and I suggested that the detailed conversations, transcribed from recordings, and the reproduction of every piece of material he had ever written might be best left out. Mr Parmanandansingh objected strenuously to this, but did agree to put his extensive records in a separate volume.

His autobiography, therefore, is much as he wrote it. I attended his funeral, interviewed his wife and listened to all the recordings I was allowed access to. In order not to intrude into his life story, I have tried to maintain a voice as close to Mr Parmanandansingh's as possible in writing the epilogues.

However, I would caution the reader that, save for romantic poetry, autobiography is the most subjective form of writing there is.

The quotes were put in after Paras's death, and I am pleased to say that he probably would not have approved of many of them.

Editor's Epilogue

Just as Paras P.'s coffin was lowered into its final resting-place, a knocking sound came from inside and his voice said, 'Make sure the grave is exactly six feet deep.'

The gravediggers screamed, turning as pale as possible for three black men and one brown. They dropped their ropes at once and backed away from the hole torn in the fresh earth.

Mrs P. smiled reassuringly through her tears. 'It's all right,' she said, 'it's just a tape recording.'

Thus, insisting on Correctness literally from the grave, did Paras P. end his days as he had lived them. It was the kind of grand gesture great men are noted for making. Besides, quite early in his career he had once marked papers for Cambridge ordinary level exams and, later (for he was never a man to rest on his laurels), advanced levels. That he does not mention this in his autobiography shows the modesty of the man, as well as his selective memory.

It was P.'s son, little Parma, who set up the tape. Paras had insisted on being buried with the pocket recorder which had been his constant companion since his twenty-fifth year. Indeed, there are some who say it was that recorder which was the basis of his fortune and career. Certainly he knew people from all walks of life and could always be depended on for the juiciest bits of gossip, whether in finance, politics, high fashion, good society or all of the above. Not that his life was without its share of controversy, though he always rose magnificently above mere gossip. Interest has been expressed in several quarters about Paras's extensive collection of recordings. Indeed, several generous offers have even been made by persons wanting to acquire the legacy of this great man. But, according to Paras's wishes, the recordings are being held in a safety deposit box for his son.

It is not surprising that Paras took his pocket tape recorder to the grave or trained his son in its use. No doubt he would have preferred his wife to see about his last message to the world. But the grieving Mrs P. could not do it. She had been sexually frustrated for so long that nothing seemed to matter now that her husband was gone and she could start looking around. Little Parma, however, was so like his father that people said P. must have spit on the sidewalk, except that P. would never have done anything so uncouth. ('I believe in God, cleanliness and couth,' P. once said, in one of his most quoted statements on the condition of Life.) So it is not surprising that P., drawing on his training in radio, recruited his son to ensure his last wish was carried out. It wouldn't have worked, though, if the service had run over twenty-five minutes, but P., drawing on his newspaper training, had written his own eulogy. In death, as in life, his timing was impeccable and Mrs P., as she wept at the graveside, was no doubt asking why P. couldn't have been the same way in bed. But this, unfortunately, is not part of training in journalism.

In any case, P.'s ploy didn't work, which was another parallel with his life. All that happened was that the gravediggers filled in the dirt in double-quick time. For all posterity would know, P. may now lie five-and-a-half feet under, instead of the six he insisted on. Superstitious to a man, the gravediggers did not seem to think Mrs P.'s explanation good or even likely.

'You never know, you know?' one of them, who had probably been reading Nietzsche, told her apologetically.

'Paras always knew,' she sobbed.

Indeed, it was the story of his life. See following pages.

Chapter One

> The glamour
> Of childish days is upon me, my manhood is cast
> Down in the flood of remembrance, I weep like a
> child for the past.
>
> From 'Piano' by D.H. Lawrence

It was the Greek philosopher Socrates – though it may have been my physician, Dr Nerahoo – who once said that the unexamined life is not worth examining. Which seems kind of obvious, so maybe Socrates said something else entirely. And if it was Dr Nerahoo, he was talking about my prostate. But I agree with both principles.

However, it is not only for this reason that I have decided to write this book, but also because of the hundreds – literally thousands – of requests I have received for a comprehensive account of my life, and how I became a household name and, later, a letter.

I shall begin at the beginning.

As a boy, I was very young. There are those who will say that this is an obstacle most, if not all, men of ambition face before, of course, they become men. But I think I was able to overcome it better than most. Even as a baby, I am told, I displayed unusual maturity and never needed to be burped. This leads me to believe that from birth my destiny was set to be a person who, almost instinctively one might say, knew correct behaviour.

3

Yet my natural propensities – some, whose names I have forgotten, have been kind enough to describe them as 'sheer genius' – were undoubtedly honed, strengthened and developed into the overpowering capacity, discipline and talent which made me, according to some other people whom I cannot at this moment recall, 'the leading exemplar of my time'.

I grew up on an estate in the outskirts of the village of Penal in south Trinidad. There are those who have theorized that it is from there I drew the letter which was later to identify me throughout the length and breadth of Trinidad and around the world. However, the reasons I became Paras P. are far deeper than that, and I will come to them in time.

We – that is, my father, my stepmother, one younger brother, one younger sister and my paternal grandmother – lived in a four-bedroom bungalow. My real mother had died when I was five.

We were, of course, highly respected in the village. Gentry, you might say. This was not only because my father had land and his own business, but because my mother had been a woman of remarkable beauty. My memories of her are vague, but there are photographs which have preserved her image. Unfortunately, some error of focusing seems to have enlarged her nose and receded her chin in all the photos, but she definitely had long blonde hair and large blue eyes, although the same error causes them to appear to bulge like 'a dead crapaud'. (These are the words of my grandmother, and I mention it to finally put to rest the scandal of why I never went to her funeral. How could I forgive a woman who slandered my mother thusly?)

My father met her – my mother, not my grandmother, whom, of course, he knew from birth – on a trip to Canada and, in a whirlwind courtship, married her in three days. I have often felt that theirs must have been an unusually passionate relationship and one which perhaps accounts for my own drive.

My grandmother, I should mention again, called my mother a 'cheap whore' – another clear untruth, since several persons in the village have often remarked on my mother's generous nature to me.

Unlike the other two children, I took after my mother in colouring and my hair was a deep brown like my father's (my father used shoe polish until the day he died). Perhaps this partly explains why I am the only distinguished member of my family.

Unfortunately, my mother was buried back in Canada so those who may be interested in making a shrine of her resting-place will be unable to do so. My father never told me exactly how she died. I think everyone, including my grandmother, was too grief-stricken at the incident. In fact, in an unusual display of sensitivity, my grandmother never used the word 'dead' in referring to her at all, but always said my mother had 'gone away'.

Still, our stepmother, a thin woman with a thin face, took good care of all of us. But I felt she always fell short of the ideal which my natural mother had represented for my father and, indeed, for myself. My stepmother was dark brown in complexion and although in heated moments – which occur in the best of relation-ships – he often called her a 'black bitch' I do not think he meant it in a negative way.

Despite my fair complexion, I was never snobbish and limed even with people who lived in wooden houses. Our house was, of course, concrete. Most of these people didn't even have a vehicle of any sort, although we had both a car and a Leyland truck. Since childhood, though I have walked with kings (or certainly some really rich men), I have always striven to retain the 'common touch'. It was one of the advantages of growing up in a rural setting among my social inferiors. I have always held that, under the bank-book, we are all brothers.

In other ways, Penal was an idyllic setting. Behind our house green fields stretched to a copse of trees where I would often go to think the thoughts that laid the foundation of my public life. Although we had neighbours on the right side, the left was an empty field through which a small, crystal stream ran. In the rainy season this stream often became a small lake. My brother, Rajpaul, was almost drowned when he was eight years old and dove from the bedroom window into the flooded stream. I was outside at the time and witnessed the entire thing, and it has always remained one of my clearest childhood memories. His form was good, and he might have become a future Greg Louganis if the incident hadn't put him off swimming for life. But then again, Rajpaul was never very bright and a good diver should always test the waters before plunging into them. Rajpaul forgot this elementary rule in diving, but his near death taught me never to do so in life.

Generally, though, I would say that my childhood was a happy one. My father never beat me more than once a week, and it is his discipline which enabled me to overcome the disadvantages of youth as early as I did. 'You not too small for licks,' he would tell me. (I think I was three at the time, though I am sure I received punishment before this.) But my father was a man who understood the need for flexibility in a truly disciplined upbringing and later, when I was thirteen, he would tell me, 'You not too big for licks.'

My father was himself one of the most disciplined men I have ever known. He would never drink alcohol on Sundays and I have even known him, during Lent or Divali or Ramadan, to forgo rum an additional day and drink only beer. In these degenerate times it is rare to find such men, both iron-willed and deeply spiritual. In fact, I find spiritual leaders now all too willing to pander to popular whim. But more on this issue later.

Though a truck-driver, landowner and, later, county councillor, my father still taught me the important lessons of life. From him I learned the virtues of ambition, commitment and boxing. 'Lead with the right,' he told me and, after receiving a cut lip, a black eye and a broken nose, it was a lesson I never forgot. It became a metaphor for my philosophy, which was what my father intended though, being a child, I did not fully appreciate it then. In fact, I almost – I will not say hated, but I was certainly very angry at my father for these hard lessons. But, grown now to man's estate, and considering how I turned out, I think it a pity that nowadays so many people ignore the traditional methods of upbringing.

My stepmother was a quiet woman except when she quarrelled about cooking, cleaning, children, money and my father staying

6

out late. She was devoted to her adopted family. My father and she had what I consider to be a good relationship and he never hit her in front of any of the children. Our meals were always ready on time, our clothes were always pressed and we were reasonably clean. My impeccable appearance, which contributed so much to my career, undoubtedly had its roots in my stepmother's training.

Well do I remember her shrill voice enjoining me, 'Get in the bathroom quick, you little wretch!' She was a firm woman, though not so firm as my father, who was a firm man. But my stepmother also had that· unsuspected softness which is so necessary for balance in a child's life. This would often come to the fore when she had been cooking with rum. Sometimes, after we had eaten the evening meal, she would say, 'You belly full?' At those times, my heart felt as though it was bursting with love, and my stomach felt the same, but with dhal, bhaji and curry duck.

Eating so well, along with my real mother's genes, undoubtedly also made a difference in my early life. You must understand that East Indian people are generally a small-boned race and often have thin calves. But being half white – and many people paid me the compliment of thinking I was fully so – I had unusually rounded calves and, in school, was able to wear shorts with pride. Perhaps I would have gotten foolishly arrogant if my waistline had not also been rounded, thus leading to jeers from my classmates. But these things are sent to test us.

Later, in my adult years, I still retained my full calves and nearly everybody had bulging waistlines. One generally wore long pants by then, of course, but I always carried within myself the knowledge that I could, if I so chose, wear shorts where lesser men would have quailed and made excuses. And does not all true strength lie within us?

So far, I have given a general outline of the family background which shaped my early perspective. But the other influence which shapes us is, of course, education.

I went to school in the two-level concrete building built by the

7

government and the Presbyterian church for the area. Although we were nominally Hindu, my father later converted in order to get a legal English name – he chose Roderick – so he could more easily win a county council seat and give himself trucking contracts. He was a very clever businessman.

It was in this school that I got my first true exposure to the gritty, seamy side of life. Here I was in daily contact with children much less fortunate, and certainly darker-complexioned. Sometimes, able as I was even at that age to relate well, I would speak to them. As I learned about their poor, often difficult lives, it gave me great comfort to think that I was not them. And I like to think that, young as I was, I inspired some of my schoolmates to try to be like me. I know several of them began staying out of the sun to avoid tanning, and it may be that several persons who today do not have skin cancer owe it to my influence.

I was, of course, the teachers' pet. I betrayed from very early on an aptitude for English. In Standard One, I could already spell 'terrible', 'whisper' and 'hurricane'. Yet insofar as education can shape one's attitude for the rest of one's life, I remember, curiously enough, an event in the arithmetic class.

Our teacher was Mr Clarke, a thick-set brown-skinned man with sideburns. He didn't beat you except when you got things wrong. Then he would hit with a hard hand to make sure it didn't happen again. I never understood why this didn't work with most of the children, because Mr Clarke's hand was *very* hard.

I only knew this by seeing the other children writhe, because I had been in his class for about two months and had never been hit. But that day we were doing long multiplication and, for the first time, I had to go to the front of the class and do the sum on the blackboard. I multiplied 3,000 by 9 and got 27,000. I distinctly remember sweating while I stood at the blackboard, waiting. Mr Clarke looked at his book, looked at me, and said, 'Correct'. It was then I realized that there is no sweeter word in the English language.

Indeed, language itself became of crucial importance to me. The

8

principal of the school, Reverend Charles, was a well-spoken man with black eyes. He was well-respected by everyone and boys who were sent to him for wrongdoing could often barely sit when they came back. I myself was greatly fearful lest he should find me attractive.

But, oh, how I admired his diction! To hear him pronounce his Os was indeed a joy most sublime. I became aware of how badly those around me spoke and, on a day that my life was changed forever, I read that the BBC announcers on the radio were considered the epitome of proper English speakers. Although this information was contained in a textbook, I could hardly credit that there were better English speakers in this world than the Reverend Charles. Obviously, though, there had to be or else God would have made him a BBC announcer instead of a mere priest.

It was with trembling fingers that I tuned in to the BBC that very night.

Listening to the lady who read the news, I realized what an immense task I faced. It was not merely the aspect of pronunciation. There was a whole quality, a whole manner, about speaking the 'Queen's English' which I realized I had to acquire. And, in what was undoubtedly the first truly mature decision of my life, I resolved to do so.

I was then eleven.

That age may seem too late to change speaking habits which were by then so firmly entrenched and, I dare say, for any lesser person it would have been. But I also had entrenched in me the iron resolve to be Correct. And if I did not speak correctly, people would not *know* I was Correct.

I do not say it was easy. Every night I listened to the BBC broadcast and repeated it word for word. Even so, it was slow going. And then inspiration struck! I began eating large quantities of green fig and drastically cut down my daily intake of water. With the resulting constipation, my accent became perfect.

By the time I was sixteen, I was certain I could have stepped into the BBC studios and they would have fallen gladly upon me, like wolves on a fatted calf. Two minor examples: I said 'in*tense*' instead, as so many people do, '*in*tense'. Thus, no one would ever have interpreted my stating that I was serious as meaning that I was occupying a canvas structure. I even said, properly, '*wim*-men' instead of the more common, and mistaken, '*wuh*-men', which no doubt accounted for my later romantic success. After all, we are how we speak.

My father, at first, was not pleased.

'Watt de fock wrong wit you?' he would say.

'No, Pa,' I would gently correct him. 'You should say: "What the fuck is wrong with you?"'

I made certain to get the proper aspirant in the 'what', the short 'uh' in 'fuck' and, of course, to pronounce my 'th' in 'with'. My father just looked at me strangely and left me alone. I think he realized I was becoming a man.

It is said that one's nature is set by the age of three. Perhaps so. But I believe that one can still make footprints in the concrete of one's self up to adolescence. Certainly, it was in this period that the path of my life was truly set as a person who always walked on the pavement and not on the road.

Ah, adolescence! The time when one begins to truly become a man, if one belongs to the male sex. With my earnest desire to overcome youth, I was quite gratified to find that, by the time I was fourteen, my facial hair had sprouted quite respectably, although it was black in colour. In fact, I could easily have been mistaken for a mature sixteen-year-old and, for this reason, was often given responsible positions – I was blackboard monitor for the entire year in Form Two – by the various teachers at my secondary school (Virgin Mary's Boys' College).

This caused some envy among the other boys, and they would often call me 'old fatso' or 'big hen'. But I think there was genuine respect behind these boyish jibes. I did not mind, because my slight – it was actually quite negligible – tendency towards plumpness marked me as a future man of substance. I also understood proper deportment to be of far more importance in one's career than athletics, and paid careful attention to walking in a calm, restrained manner. The rash caused by my thighs rubbing together I thought a small price to pay.

But the fact is, I *was* a teenager and could not altogether escape the hormonal fate of those years. One is subject to so many strange and powerful impulses, and I was no exception.

For the first time, I shall speak of it.

The strange, wondrous and appalling impulse descended upon me in my fourteenth year. Perhaps if I had had any inkling of what was to occur I might have had time to prepare. But temptation came like a thunderbolt out of a blue sky.

I had always been aware, of course, of the temptations around me. But I was immune to their blandishments. Every lunchtime I, along with hundreds of other boys, would invade the main street to view delights beyond the reach of hand, but not imagination.

And then my father, who had just become a councillor and awarded himself a lucrative contract to carry water for the government, began giving me pocket money.

I might have resisted. But, remember, although I had been battling against it, I was still young.

The day after I received my first allowance, I went with the more experienced boys and bought a chocolate bar. And so the shame began.

It was only when I actually began eating chocolate that I realized the impulse had always been present within me – deeply buried, it is true, but waiting to flare out like an uncontrollable forest fire.

I think I had liked chocolate even at age eleven. Certainly, I remember, before I even knew chocolate was made from cocoa, sugar and lecithin, looking at the gaily wrapped bars on the candy counter at the grocery and getting strangely weak at the knees.

But, at fourteen, my real education began. I learned that the Amerindian word for cocoa was *cacao*. So thorough was my

11

research, I even learned that they had made a drink from it. In my defence, I can say only that I was a precocious child. Also, let me hasten to add that I never ate all the chocolate I *could* have. When I tell you that I even knew chocolate contained phenythelamine, but did nothing about it, you will understand my relative restraint. Many grown men, I like to think, could not have done so well.

But I nibbled. Oh, how I nibbled! I seemed to like living on the edge. I knew phenythelamine stimulated the production of endorphins which create feelings of utter satisfaction, but did I care? In a word, no.

Only once in that black period did I manage to quit briefly. That was when I developed a serious crush on Hayley Mills after watching *Pollyanna*. For a time, the madness seemed to pass while I dreamed about meeting Hayley, collected photographs of her, and imagined what she was like in real life. But, in the end, true love proved a poor substitute for real chocolate. As the old saying so aptly goes, a woman is only a woman but chocolate is pleasure. I was soon back at the candy counter.

Only one person ever discovered my guilty secret – my sister Kamini, who came into the room unexpectedly just as I had unwrapped a new bar.

I was mortified but, although only twelve, she treated the matter quite matter-of-factly. Females seem to acquire such maturity quite automatically, and lose it only if they're forty, single and desperate.

Kamini suggested that I needed some other outlet for my energies.

'You should get married,' she said, 'or try transcendental meditation.'

But I was stubborn.

'I don't want to share my chocolate,' I said, 'and my teeth are fine.'

Yet I had to admit that my habit had gotten out of hand. Some days, I would find myself eating three meals of chocolate and having food for dessert. Perhaps if I could have hidden the effects, I might never have overcome my addiction. My teeth were all right, but the same could hardly be said for my skin.

Pimple city was a spreading metropolis on the previously unblemished map of my face. At first, these eruptions provided amusement and even relief. Many a night I would stand in front of my mirror and burst them one after the other. I would grab a pinch of skin between thumb and forefinger, and squeeze until a small white blob erupted prettily. Sometimes, I stuck a plastic bullseye on the mirror and made target practice. On other nights, I tried for distance, although that was rather painful since it required a hard squeeze and, for best results, a pimple that was not *quite* ripe . . . but I don't suppose you are really interested in all this.

Suffice to say, that all this activity began to take its toll, as overtraining always must. (I had developed quite agile and strong fingers by this time – a skill which served me well in my later career in journalism and which also explains why so many journalists are pockmarked wonders.)

Perhaps only those who have had good complexions can fully appreciate the trauma I faced. Like a forest which has been overcut, my pimples began leaving raw red pustules on my face. Now when people looked at me, they did not see my fair skin, but red blisters.

But I learned a valuable lesson from this: that most people see only the obvious. I began to appreciate those who saw beyond the surface, who looked beyond my pimples and saw my skin for what it truly was.

Nobody, of course, knew about my chocolate consumption, but people were beginning to wonder what was going on. Even my father expressed concern in his usual gruff but kindly manner: 'Gyad, boy, wash your face, nah,' he told me.

I realized it was not enough to stop bursting my pimples. I would have to stop getting pimples entirely – in other words, give up chocolate. But was I strong enough?

13

At this crucial crossroads in my life, along came Father Royd.

At the time I attended it, the Virgin's Boys' College consisted of two buildings. The older segment was a long, two-level structure with arches which, in its simple austerity, made me think of a cell block although, on some evenings when the soft light of the westering sun caught the building just right, it looked like a giant coffin instead.

I spent Forms One to Four in this building – my formative years, you might say – and it was in Form Three, in the fourth period, that I first heard Father Herman Royd speak. And, although I did not realize it at the time, the seed was planted which was later to flower into a major stem of my life.

It was just by chance – I now know it was destiny – that Father Royd happened to take our class that day. We were supposed to have Spanish, but the teacher had not come. Father Royd, who happened to be visiting the school as he often did, came to hold on. It was the one time in my life I was grateful for the general indiscipline which was so constant around me.

I have sometimes thought about the train of events since then. Suppose the Spanish teacher had come, or suppose Father Royd had not been in school at that precise time, or suppose the other boys had not been throwing paper? I might never have heard him speak, might never even have become Paras P. This is why I truly believe, as Shakespeare so elegantly put it, that there is a divinity which shapes our ends, though faithless people choose to rely on devices such as the ButtClencher instead.

Father Royd was a tall, thin man. When he sat, he immediately brought to mind one of those clever rulers which fold into three sections and slip neatly into your pocket. He had large teeth and an expressionless face which, I later realized, conveyed an unearthly calm (the face, I mean, not the teeth, which just suggested a good dental plan).

To quiet us down, the Father began lecturing on a subject he knew would catch our attention: masturbation. Like most of the other boys, I listened with a mixture of embarrassment, interest and excitement. But, unlike with them, there was no prurience in any of these feelings with me.

Father Royd termed masturbation 'the besetting sin of teenagers'. But he hastened to point out that some adults also indulged in this reprehensible act. It amazed me that anyone could talk on a subject like this so easily, so knowledgeably and, most importantly, with such passionate conviction.

Conviction! That was what held me spellbound. As Father Royd spoke, his burning yet expressionless gaze rested on each boy in turn. Few could meet those direct, honest eyes. He licked his lips often, yet never paused to go for a drink of water. By the time he was finished, he was even sweating. What strength this man had, I felt!

I never felt a sharper regret than when the bell rang to signal the period's end. Father Royd, too, blinked as though coming out of a light trance and admonished us to do what God wanted us to do, no matter what religion we belonged to.

I reached home that evening with my mind in a whirl. The glimpse of such deep belief, such unshakeable conviction, such calm power, had impressed me profoundly. Up to that time, there had only been one true passion in my life. Now I had glimpsed something which seemed at least equally strong as a love for chocolate. It seemed hard to credit, yet I was convinced that, were Father Royd to be offered unlimited chocolate, he would be able to refuse it without a second thought.

The timing of Father Royd's entry into my perspective was also significant. By this time, I had begun to realize the bad effects of chocolate. Even backyard mud, recognized by most leading obeah women as the best means for getting smooth unblemished skin, did not work for me. But in religion, I felt, I might find an eternal cure for acne.

Simplistic, you say? Perhaps in a way it was. Yet are not all fundamental truths simple ones? What *is* acne, but corruption of the skin? Might it not be that in striving for inner purity I might attain smoothness of skin, and save myself a fortune in dermatological treatments? Didn't the Bible speak of 'oil to maketh his face shine', proving that clear skin was a blessed quality?

It is true the Hindu culture I was brought up in offered much. At *yagnas*, for example, I could eat food off fig-leaves with my fingers. But I craved something more.

Thus, at a quite young age, I began studying religion deeply. I discovered many truths about life, but also many things that puzzled me. Hinduism suggested, for example, that God was a vegetarian. I could see this as being plausible, and even as a help to my acne, for why else would God have invented spinach, broccoli and watercress?

But, on the other hand, Muslims argued that God liked meat once you asked His permission to kill it. Fine. Yet the Muslims also insisted that God didn't like pork, and this I didn't understand. Was it believable, I asked myself, that God would invent something like pigs unless they were ultimately meant to be converted into bacon?

I have never really trusted Islam since then.

I even turned briefly to philosophy to find answers to the eternal mysteries. Does a chair exist if we are not aware of it? I remember waking up in the middle of a moonless night to go and urinate. On the way there, I tripped over a chair, fell flat on my face, and burst about three pimples at once. And I thought: if you can trip over an unseen chair, the chair *must* exist!

I continued making such unusually stubborn efforts to think clearly. Even my subconscious self got into the act, and I would work out philosophical conundrums in my dreams. One night, after reading the *Dialogues*, I dreamt of Socrates arguing that even though a chair is destroyed, it still exists because the idea of a chair still exists in the heads and bottoms of all sitting people.

But this concept infuriated Socrates's wife all the more, she just having thrown the chair in question at his head in the midst of a domestic dispute. He had been trying to pretend he didn't care if she took the axe to all the furniture. So she did.

I dreamed that Plato dropped by later and asked Socrates why the furniture was now firewood. Socrates repeated his argument and invited Plato to have a seat. But Plato just looked at him strangely and said, 'Thanks, but I've got to see a man about a dog.'

It is my strength as a philosopher which accounts for much of my later success. But even more significant than that was my personal relationship with God, which also began around this time. In fact, He would often invite me to have dinner with Him. Naturally, all this was conducted on a spiritual plane but, apart from that, we were never very formal.

It was easy to tell the difference between my dreams and these genuine visions. God, as you might expect, was an entertaining companion and always served very good wine. Sacramental, I believe. When I was merely dreaming, I never got refreshments. And there were always revelations. I remember Him telling me once the story of His first meal. It seemed that he had just had a hard day – the sixth, I believe, when He created the Earth's creatures – and He was tired and hungry and there was no one to bring Him food. That was when the idea of creating a creature to serve Him faithfully came to Him.

'Just like that,' He said, snapping His fingers.

He said He knew He would have to give the creature hands, so it wouldn't drop the dishes. 'But then I remembered I had already made the monkey,' said God. 'So I realized I needed a creature which had enough brains not to swing from trees, or else my meals would have been cold by the time they reached Me.'

'You needed a creature smart enough to handle a delivery service,' I said.

'Exactly,' said God, nodding. 'So I put some of My essence into this creature, and called him Man since dog was taken already. But Man started dropping all my meals, and I found that his wrist was stiff from overuse and his back weak from lack of use. So I had to invent Woman. But then Man and Woman, who had free will because My divinity was within them, began mating at all

17

seasons. So I cast them out of My celestial kitchen and said, "Go forth and multiply." I knew they would do it anyway, you see.'

I always awoke from these visions with a feeling of complete satisfaction, and often wanting to smoke a cigarette. So I knew from an early age that I had a unique destiny.

Chapter Two

The pen! foredoomed to aid the mental throes
Of brains that labour, big with verse or prose.

From *English Bards and Scotch
Reviewers – a Satire* by Lord Byron

So far my life had been mostly theory. It was when I entered university that I truly found myself struggling with life's hard realities.

The university was a place where one went to acquire a higher education. If you applied yourself conscientiously, you learned how to make more money than the majority of the population. At the time I was there, enrolment was only about six per cent of all persons with secondary education. We have made considerable progress since then, largely because, with the economy the way it is, the government has had to remove several subsidies, thus blocking tertiary education to the poorer classes. This, naturally, has ensured greater efficiency in the education system for, as more than one authority has pointed out, tertiary education is wasted on the lower classes. Not only do they usually waste their learning and become socialists, but they rarely know how to choose good wines.

However, this is not the place to pontificate since my readers, I am sure, are more interested in knowing of the struggles, and triumphs, I experienced at the university.

And what struggles, and triumphs, they were! For the first time in my life, I found myself with no social advantages. Nearly everyone in the university was at least as well off as I. Some had parents in business or in high government posts. Even those who were there on scholarships, as is usually the case, already had loads of money.

You may wonder if my complexion did not single me out for special attention. The answer is, no. Besides the fact that the stress of university life caused my skin to be hidden under a rash of pimples, there was a higher proportion of fair people in university than I had ever encountered in Penal. There were even a few foreign students who were as white as milk.

Having my cloistered, idyllic world so suddenly ripped away was, as you might imagine, a profound shock. But it was then that my innate breeding truly told. A lesser person might have crumbled under such drastic change, might even have quit the university. But I resolved to face up to my new challenges and, yes, overcome them. As Ernest Hemingway once said, the true test of a true man is his ability to turn obstacles into stumbling-blocks. Or was that Woody Allen?

At any rate, I put my nose to the grindstone. The reader may ask what resources, in my naked and assailed state, did I have to fall back on? There is an old saying that we are never given more than we can handle, though this does not apply to husbands. But I agree that, if we have faith in ourselves, we generally find we have the resources to deal with anything.

I said earlier that I entered university without any advantages. But that is not exactly true. There was one thing on which I could rely through all my travails. I refer, of course, to my hair.

I have mentioned before that I had brown hair. But, in dismissing my hair so lightly, I may have given the reader the impression that my hair was a dull, mousy brown – the kind of hair, in other words, which makes no difference to the scalp it grows on.

If so, I must apologize. It is the cross of the biographer that, in relating the details of a richly spent life, one often ignores certain details only later to realize their crucial importance in the scheme of things. (One could perhaps philosophize at considerable length on Life and even cooking at this juncture, but perhaps not.)

To set the record of history straight, then, my hair was thick, wavy and gleamed lustrously when I applied coconut oil. Indeed, on the first day I entered university, I noticed several people, among them some not unattractive young women, turn as I passed and begin whispering among themselves, as though asking 'Who is he?' In later life, I was to become quite used to this, but at the time I was still unaccustomed to such attention. I might say, however, that the pleasure never diminished. Indeed, on that same day, many a person I passed drew a sharp breath and looked at me. Perhaps it was my natural nobility of bearing – my deportment was, of course, perfected by this age and no longer resulted in inner thigh rashes – but undoubtedly the attention paid to my gleaming hair also accounted for it.

This gave me the confidence to face university life. At times, as Dr Nerahoo often told me, we all need a shot in the butt. Father Royd, I recall, also said the same thing.

In order to fully understand the course of my life, however, I should give you some idea of my studies.

Bearing in mind the ultimate aims of higher education, and my innate sense of social reponsibility, I had intended to do either Law or Business Management. But, for technical reasons I need not go into (but which, I suspect to this day, involved political resentment of my father), I was unable to enter either faculty.

I instead went into the Faculty of General Studies – a decision which, as it turned out, was to bode well for my future public life.

My courses began. Undoubtedly, the three most important areas of study I took, which were later to affect fundamentally the courses of both my private and public lives, were Literature107, Economics100 and Sewing911. I found myself taking to academia, if I may coin a phrase, like a fish to water. The university life, it seemed, suited my sensitive and intellectual temperament.

I began to grow strong in spirit.

Indeed, this was one of the first things that distinguished me

21

from the other undergraduates. To cope with their courses, many of them turned to vodka or even brandy. But my father's training stood me in good stead, and I found rum adequate for all my needs.

It was not that I had anything against vodka, brandy or even scotch. But there were certain principles to which I felt I should adhere: rum was locally made and it was cheaper. Too many of my colleagues, I felt, ignored their wider economic and, indeed, patriotic responsibilities. It seems a harsh thing to say of those who were supposed to be the intelligentsia, and future leaders of the Caribbean, but the fact is that they seemed hardly to care what they drank, once it wasn't plain orange juice.

Yet here I ran into a contradiction. Even at that relatively youthful age, I was not against free trade. Adam Smith echoed many of my own ideas. I found myself with that dilemma which virtually every young man, at this stage in life, faces: how to resolve patriotic fervour with economic beliefs. I realized then that my philosophy of Correctness, which I had already begun to formulate, would need to be expanded.

I had, simplistically and naively, put the blame on politics. Yet the government had only recently passed anti-dumping legislation. They could not be blamed because vodka, champagne, even Irish whiskey, entered our shores freely, often duty free.

Certainly, there was typical bureaucratic inefficiency. But only when I began researching the subject did I appreciate the true magnitude of the problem our society faced.

Dumping, I discovered, was an issue even older than bureaucracy. For example, a loose translation I did of ancient Egyptian hieroglyphics from the tomb of Rameses II says: '. . . and Cleopatra had sexual congress with Mark Anthony and her loins were as honey . . . So it was she left Caesar who therewith became very depressed and had to see his therapist.'

This provided me with considerable food for thought. Who knows how dumping may have contributed to the decline and fall of the Roman empire? Indeed, it is my own theory that the entire

22

history of Western civilization might have been different had Cleopatra faced stiff penalties for dropping Caesar like a hot potato.

But, in the absence of necessary legislation, decadence slowly but surely crept into civilization and, if we are to believe Chaucer, apparently was even invited to all the best parties. By the Middle Ages, I found in my reading, there was ample evidence of this trend.

For example, Chaucer in the 14th century describes the Wife of Bath as 'a worthy womman all hir lyve:/Housbondes at chirche dore she hadde fyve'. Why the rush? For the sake of decency, surely she could have waited until they got home. With that attitude, it's no wonder all her husbands kicked the bucket, yet she was never prosecuted for her flagrant sexual abuse and would not be even today. Instead, she was described as a 'worthy womman' and mention is hardly made of the long-suffering Mr Bath.

I was next tempted to make blame more specific and criticize the Customs Department. Yet, as I came to Shakespeare in Lit107, I found I had come in late here, too. Four hundred years ago, the bard had written: 'Age cannot wither her nor custom stale/Her infinite variety'. Learning to read metaphors, I understood, of course, that Shakespeare was referring to the amount of goods customs officers have to deal with from women who have been on overseas shopping trips. Women were simply too much for the average customs officers, and there are no above-average customs officers.

With such a weight of history behind it, I realized that the best-drafted anti-dumping legislation would prove a light counterbalance indeed. I could not say what the future held. The aerobics classes were fully booked, yet Economics100 showed me that the chocolate market had not declined. There needed to be, I thought, a mathematical formula worked out to explain the connection between chocolate, acne and girdles. But who was to do it? Certainly not a Third World university.

By this, I do not mean to imply no useful research went on at the university. But academicians were hampered by all sorts of problems which persons in developed countries did not face.

Lecturers at the university, for example, were often accused by those outside of living in an ivory tower. I know for a fact that this accusation was baseless. Most of the lecturers actually lived in the rent-free bungalows attached to the campus.

The trouble was, the wider society never attempted to take advantage of the research carried out by university lecturers. Indeed, studies were often stymied by the limited minds of those who did not appreciate academia. My economics professor, Dr M. Bagshott, had, for example, begun work on a model proving Caribbean economies could develop faster if women received more tuition. He even outlined an entire paradigm which proved the model herself could make it big on the international stage. Unfortunately, he had to cancel the project when his wife found out.

Would this have happened in an advanced country? I think not. But the need for research is not well appreciated here.

Yet, for all that, the intellectual life at the university was extremely stimulating for one who, like myself, had always enjoyed thinking. When I tell you that many mornings I leaped out of bed at the crack of nine o'clock – often having stayed up the previous night until ten – you will understand how fully I threw myself into my studies.

Well do I remember my first lecture! It was Lit107 and we were introduced to the Caribbean's leading poet: Derek Walcott. (I believe he won some sort of prize many years later. It's always nice winning prizes. I won a bottle of Peardrax once at a hoopla stall and the sense of triumph has always stayed with me.)

Our lecturer was Professor Arman, who was actually a woman. It was the first time I realized that there were female professors – I knew they existed, of course, but I had always thought they were called something else. She had, she said, actually met Mr Walcott. This interested me tremendously, because I had never seen some-

24

one who had actually met someone else who had written a book. Of course, my wonder was tempered by the fact that poetry collections aren't really books except in a technical sense.

Still, Professor Arman seemed terribly impressed: 'I consider Walcott the greatest poet, living and dead, in the world today,' she said.

This puzzled the class considerably, since it did not seem likely that Walcott could be both. One or the other, surely. But I suppose, inasmuch as he won a prize, he must have been alive and pretty well respected even by those who hadn't met him. I read some of his poetry myself and didn't understand a word of it so he must have been pretty good. Thank God for *Concise Literature Notes*, though – or rather, thank Mr Concise, wherever he rests – which allowed us not to read the texts but still answer examination questions as if we had. I have always held that the true test of intelligence is the ability to talk or write well on issues you know absolutely nothing about. This ability was to serve me well when I entered the hurly-burly of political life in later years.

Before that, however, I discovered that there were serious questions in life which had nothing to do with either money, chocolate or skin. There was, I found, a whole world of intellectual effort labouring to solve some of life's eternal mysteries – a disinterested, yet passionate, and somehow noble odyssey.

These questions spanned the entire range of human endeavour. Who wrote the works of Shakespeare? Did dark matter exist? How do they get the holes in macaroni?

In Lit107, we discussed the mystery of Shakespeare's writing with great avidity. Even from my secondary school days, I remember seeing the name William Shakespeare printed on the cover of my texts. But there was a school of thought – not at Virgin's Boys' College, obviously – which held that this was but a clever forgery. Handwriting experts through the centuries had been able to make little progress. We discussed this matter thoroughly, but reached no conclusions. This in itself was a political education.

The issue of dark matter arose in one of my general courses, which was supposed to educate us on pressing topics of the day. It was, I admit, an issue which disturbed me profoundly. I had read Einstein's *Theory of General Relativity*, but this said nothing about the subject. Perhaps it would have if, like a truly great man such as the Prophet Mohammed, he had written a Specific Theory of Absoluteness. As it was, I was thrown back on my own intellectual resources, which I rapidly exhausted.

Did dark matter? To tell the truth, I couldn't see that it did. Everywhere we heard about America, Britain, Europe. Without these white countries, what would civilization have been? They had given us hamburgers, Coke, music videos.

Africa, on the other hand, didn't seem to be doing anything lately except having famines, droughts, wars and various diseases. There was no entertainment value there, unless you had a really sick mind. Even Asia was producing toasters, cassette players and televisions, and nearly everyone was Oriental. How then, I reasoned, could dark matter? And if it did not matter did it truly exist? Even chairs, we know, are for sitting on. I do not say I found my conclusions palatable. I just say I could find no fault with my logic.

As for the holes in macaroni, I never did find out how this is done. It remains, I suppose, one of the great unsolved mysteries.

All this does not mean that I spent all my time at university in contemplative thought and study. To be quite frank, given the number of attractive young women at the university, that would have been impossible for any normal, hot-blooded male human being, and I must say I found it difficult myself.

There seemed to be more women than men at the university, although this was unlikely. Perhaps I had this impression just because the women were more obvious. It has always seemed to me that women have this natural capacity to be decorative. You see it in the way they wear their hair, their clothes, their jewellery and even the shoes on their feet.

Men, of course, only look distinguished in three-piece suits or silver-grey hair. And it was in this regard that I faced my most difficult challenge.

My hair, as I have mentioned, was brown. I did wear three-piece suits on campus initially, but had to stop because of the heat. Having to wear long-sleeved shirts or shirt jacks instead was a very traumatic experience. Even wearing the occasional two-piece suit only eased my mental agony at falling short of my true potential. It was a great trial but, luckily, I was taking Sewing as one of my electives, and this helped ease the strain.

Even so, my suffering was not purposeless. How true it is we are tempered by adversity! For, were it not for this situation, I might never have understood the Correctness of countries with temperate climates.

I was not a snobbish person. In fact, I often said hello to people who attended the same classes I did, and I did so without regard to race, colour or financial position. However, I was careful about the people with whom I socialized. Even at that stage of my life, you see, I knew that some day my background might come in for close scrutiny.

I did make it a point to talk to the foreigners at the university. I felt that they would appreciate a friend in a strange country and one should, after all, always try to learn about other cultures. The United States, Britain and Canada, I found, were quite fascinating countries. (Unfortunately, I did not find as much time to speak to foreign students from Africa, India or even the other Caribbean islands.)

But, speaking to my friends from the metropole made me even more aware of the limitations of my clothing. In their temperate climate, my close friends could have worn three-piece suits every day of their lives. And then it hit me! Men from the United States, Britain or Canada were more attractive to our women, not because they were white or spoke proper English – though these were certainly points in their favour – but because of their habit of wearing suits.

There is, after all, an innate admiration for well-cut clothes in

27

every civilized human being. If nakedness were not a sin, we would have invented clothes anyway. I remember reading someone once – probably a biblical scholar – who said that when the Word became flesh, the first thing it did was get dressed so people would take it seriously. A good point.

But there was another reason why the female students distracted me. The fact is, the women at the university were unlike any others I had ever encountered in my twenty years. Difficult as it may be for those who have not experienced the academic lifestyle, nearly all the women on campus went around clutching books in their arms.

In plain view.

I understood, of course, that this was part of university life. Yet even so it struck me that most of these young women, more independent than their less educated sisters, chose not to carry books in their bags. In fact, even those who did use bags loaded them so heavily that it was quite obvious what they were carrying. Maybe even more so. Such bags, to my mind, almost shouted, 'Look! I have a mind!'

Every day, then, I was subjected to the sight of young, obviously intelligent women, carrying three or four textbooks. Often hardcover. Many also carried ring folders. And there were two or three, usually surrounded by a herd of male students, who owned binders covered in genuine leather.

Inevitably, my chocolate consumption increased.

That women could display their minds so casually – I might even say wantonly – was a revelation to one of my sheltered upbringing in Penal. And I cannot tell a lie: I found it stimulating.

In my defence, I can say only that I was very young. And I think, for my age, I conducted myself with commendable discipline. Had I been a typically lax young man, I would have undoubtedly found myself in the University Bar every evening drinking beer and talking about women and, perhaps, even *to* them. This, I am proud to say, never happened. Instead, I went to

28

the bar only on Wednesdays, Thursdays and Fridays and I drank only rum.

Nor, as I say, did I speak to the women who came in. The reader may perhaps be shocked to learn that members of the fairer sex – though, as I have pointed out, I was just as fair as anyone – actually came into the bar. But it should be appreciated that the University Bar was not simply a place where people came to drink. It was really a forum – although, as I say, they also had beer – for ideas. It was a place for a meeting of the minds, not just drinking, smoking, card-playing, necking or taking marijuana.

Indeed, some of the most stimulating and thought-provoking conversations I have ever heard took place right on the well-worn seats of the bar stools in the smoke-filled dimness of that University Bar.

We discussed issues both local, regional and international, like the seven o'clock newscast. In a very real way, it was these discussions which laid the foundation for my future career in the media and in drinking. The range of topics was wide, as suited young, curious and often brilliant minds. Women's rights, health care, economic success, cancer, the longest length of time you could leave potato salad without bringing it to life – everything was grist for our mill (whatever grist is). I always took copious notes at these discussions and, looking back, find I recorded many fascinating conversations. As I read my notes, I see them all once again in my mind's eye.

There was Rajesh S., for example, who was later to work with Trinidad's most famous fashion designer Choo Choo Chu, holding forth to a large group about the problems women face. Rajesh was a thin, intense young man with beautiful gestures. The rest of us sat and listened as he spoke with great eloquence about why he would not want to be a woman.

'Don't get me wrong. I like women,' he said. 'But their lives are so complex. You have to spend an extra half-hour every morning putting on make-up. If it wasn't for that, I think I'd consider it.

29

After all, I'd make a lovely woman, especially if I had less jaw and forehead, and shaved regularly.'

One of my closest friends, Brandon North, an American who was doing a research project for his master's degree, said, 'But many women nowadays don't shave regularly.'

North was like that – able to go to the heart of any topic with one incisive comment.

'True,' said Rajesh, 'and some of them look really fine with moustaches.'

'A woman was trying to seduce me last month,' said another member of the group, Wilson, thoughtfully. He was a well-built young man. 'She actually wasn't doing too badly until I saw her in a short skirt. Jungle city, man. I left, doubletime.'

'That wasn't very nice,' said Tricia Chen, the only female there.

Wilson shrugged. 'I know, and I don't blame the girl. My fault entirely. I can't stand hairy spiders, either.'

'Oh, in that case,' said Tricia, waving a hand with the confidence of a Chinese woman who knows hair grows on her body only where it's supposed to.

'But that's exactly what I'm speaking about,' said Rajesh. 'If I were a woman, I'd have to tolerate such inanities from men every day. I'd get worn out having to deal with them.'

'Women have changed in significant ways now, though,' said Tricia. 'We look at men's butts now. We know we're good in bed.'

'Women have been good in bed before,' said North who, as a man from a country with a thriving economy, knew these things.

'Yes,' said Tricia. 'But now we're proud of it.'

'The essence of good sex is cooperation,' said North, who had been exposed to *Sesame Street* much earlier than any of us.

'I'd like to talk with you about that a little more,' said Tricia, and she and North got up and left. It was often the way – our topics changed so rapidly that people usually continued them one-on-one as the crowd shifted and changed.

According to my notes, another topic which often came up was, of course, economic advancement. It was C. Ramgoolie, a part-time student who worked days, who posed the interesting question, 'If time is money, why aren't I richer?'

Aristotle Onassis, he pointed out, also had twenty-four hours in his day. Yet Onassis's day ended with him several million dollars wealthier.

'My day,' said Ramgoolie gloomily, 'ends with bills.'

He said he had sat in a bank for two hours and, at the end of that time, he was no richer than before.

'Weren't the female tellers pretty?' Wilson asked.

'Some,' he agreed.

'Well, then you were enriched inside.'

'Spiritual wealth,' Ramgoolie pointed out acidly, 'is not a negotiable quantity.'

'Unless you run a small church,' Wilson replied.

He was an excellent debater, and Ramgoolie conceded the point.

'Well, why don't you open one?' I asked Ramgoolie.

'Can't do the accent,' Ramgoolie explained.

We all nodded understandingly. It is so often the little things which prevent financial success.

'It seems to me,' said Wilson, 'that the real secret is to use your time productively.'

North, who was also there, said, 'I have some ideas on that, but few women I meet are willing to contemplate them. If you ask me, it's this unwillingness to take risks which keeps the GNP down.'

'Maybe you don't present your case convincingly enough,' Wilson suggested.

North shrugged. 'I've worn boxer shorts and used hand puppets. What more can a man do?'

Tricia, who had been silent up to this point, leaned across and whispered something in North's ear. They immediately got up and left. I have never known two people who shared such a passion for intellectual discussions.

Ramgoolie, who had been thinking about North's comment,

said, 'I see. What I've been doing wrong is spending time doing a lot when I should be saving time doing very little. That is how most rich people live, after all.'

'It's also how unemployed people live,' Wilson pointed out.

'Perhaps economics really has no solutions,' I said. I usually preferred just to listen at these discussions, but occasionally I would give the benefit of my unique insights.

'So what do you suggest, Holyface?' said Wilson. (This was their affectionate nickname for me, a reference to my spiritual air.)

'Psychiatry. Time, after all, is subjective,' I pointed out, bringing the discussion back to its original point. 'Dr Spock has even suggested that, as we get older, time contracts for us.'

'That's unlikely,' Ramgoolie said. 'As far as I know, time is infinite and would hardly need a hitman.'

I remember shrugging, thus ending the discussion. As was so often the case, I knew I was Correct. And Ramgoolie never did become rich, though I did, which, I think, speaks for itself.

Chapter Three

Nay, if you read this line, remember not
The hand that writ it; for I love you so,
That I in your sweet thoughts would be forgot,
If thinking on me then should make you woe.

From Sonnet LXXI by William
Shakespeare

I met Selina, the first great love of my life, in my second year at university.

By this time, I was quite well known about campus. I was an active member of the Students' Guild and did much useful work. Having got free trips to many of the islands in the course of my duties, I also considered myself a well-travelled man of the world. With maturity had also come the disappearance of nearly all my pimples. The scars they left behind gave me an appearance of toughness which women liked. Strange that despite all our civilization, we still retain these judgements of a more primitive era. For example, all right-thinking men want a morally upright, well-comported woman to wed, yet most men also prefer a morally upright, well-comported woman with large breasts.

Be that as it may, the young woman for whom I fell was, strangely enough, in none of these categories. But she and I were remarkably similar.

Selina Hosein was short and fair in complexion, with clear brown eyes. She also had brown hair and an aristocratic nose. She spoke English of a remarkable purity and had full calves. The explanation for these things was, as it turned out, easily found. Her father was a Muslim Indian and her mother a white Briton.

Perhaps I knew these things instinctively, because the fourth time I saw Selina, I fell completely, hopelessly in love. Only later, as our relationship developed, did I find out the details of her background. It seemed to confirm for me that we were twin souls, or at least very compatible. But this knowledge did not make my courtship an easy task.

Many outstanding men in their younger years have suffered from a painful shyness. I was no exception. Despite my public role on campus, I found it difficult to communicate with people save in an official capacity or, in extreme circumstances, with hand puppets. I had noticed Selina but, since she was quite flat-chested and carried a knapsack, she did not really attract more than my casual attention. I liked the way she carried her nose, but by itself that was not enough to fire my passions. I have often found that we initially overlook those who affect us the most, just as we initially ignore those who don't affect us at all. There is a lesson there, although I don't know what it is.

But, in one day, I heard Selina speak and saw her in shorts. From that moment I was a lost man.

Until that day, I had foolishly assumed she was just a fair East Indian. Her upper body was quite slim and, until the morning she came into the Guild in shorts, I had naturally assumed her legs also were slim.

This was not the case. Her calves, to my shock, were full and rounded. If her eyes had been slanted, I might even have thought she was Chinese. Then she spoke.

'I want to buy a university T-shirt.'

Every perfectly pronounced word pealed in my brain like the rich, silver tones of some golden bell. I fell in love in between 'I' and 'T-shirt'. Romeo, I believe, had a similar experience with Juliet, except he liked her glove.

34

Had we been in a social situation, I might have gaped at her for several minutes. But I was on duty in the Guild, and my rigorous training automatically took over.

'What size do you take?' I asked, pronouncing all five words correctly though in a slightly strangled manner.

'Medium,' she said.

The word had never sounded sweeter. I had a sudden, urgent desire to hear her order steak.

'And what colour do you like?' I asked, controlling myself with a Herculean effort.

'What do you have?'

Until that moment I had managed to remain professional and dispassionate. But now I shot her a hot glance.

'White,' I said, boldly adding, 'my dear.'

'Fine,' she said.

I pulled out a medium T-shirt from under the counter, and as I handed it over and took her money I realized this extraordinary girl was about to walk out of my day. I searched desperately for something to say.

'You know, I'm also white,' I said.

She paused.

'Excuse me?' she said.

Sweat broke out on my brow.

'Uh, I'm also white,' I stammered. 'Well, half-white. Like the T-shirt. Sort of.' I changed the topic desperately. 'Aren't you white, too?'

I blushed a little as I realized, in my nervousness, I had used two contractions in five seconds. To my relief, she seemed not to have noticed.

'What's your name?' she asked.

I brightened at once. She was interested!

'Paras Parmanandansingh,' I said.

'I see,' she said pleasantly. She leaned on the counter, and I felt dizzy at having her face so close to mine. 'Tell me, Paras. Are you an idiot?'

'No,' I answered, relieved she had asked an easy one.

'Well,' she said, 'you give an excellent impression of one.'

I was bathed in confusion at this unexpected praise. I had never considered mimicry to be among my varied talents, yet this intelligent girl had perceived it at once.

'What is your name?' I stammered.

'I suppose you'd find out, anyway, wouldn't you?'

'I have access to Guild records,' I said, trying not to sound boastful.

'My name is Selina,' she said.

'Nice to meet you,' I said, trying out a phrase I had frequently heard North employ.

'I wish I could say the same,' she said, with becoming modesty. It was perfectly obvious she could speak almost as well as I. But her womanly modesty prevented her from saying so. My love for Selina deepened even more in that moment.

'You can,' I said, with a catch in my throat.

She mumbled something I didn't quite hear and turned and left the Guild office.

I knew something good had begun.

Love affects different people in different ways. Some climb mountains, but Trinidad has only hills and in any case I have always held physical exercise to be the expression of a shallow mind. Between exercise and having premarital sex was, I felt, but a short step.

Though I was only twenty-one, the lifestyle at university left me in no doubt that many people in love often have sex, as if love was sufficient excuse for physical coupling. To such persons I posed one simple moral query: are we human beings or are we railway cars? I determined to do the Correct thing, and express my love for Selina in a proper and spiritual fashion. That very afternoon, while still at the Guild office, I recorded our first meeting while it was still fresh in my mind. Inspiration was bubbling within me like the mud volcanos at Devil's Woodyard and, in my apartment that night, I pulled out pen and paper and a bottle of rum and sat down to express my feelings in verse. Like Wordsworth, I also had bread and cheese.

The poetry I wrote in that first flush has never been published until now. Readers will perhaps criticize me for not sharing these moving lines previously, but my first taste of true love was a deeply personal experience.

The first poem I wrote, expressing my dreams, hopes and desires, used a form I knew to be very popular among poets – the immortal limerick. It went as follows:

> There was a beautiful young lady named Selina
> And like a heavenly vision I hath seen her
> Silent upon a peak in Darien;
> One day I pray I shall be carrying
> Her lunch tray in the cantina.

For my second poem, in which I expressed my admiration for Selina's unique features, I used the standard sonnet. Shakespeare, I believe, had done something similar.

> The brightness of thy smile puts the sun to shame,
> The sparkle of thine eyes to jewels does the same,
> Thy brows are unsurpassed in character,
> And thy nose hath no tata.
> Like fine brown flame is thy hair,
> And silk's fineness to thine skin cannot compare;
> Thy spiritual qualities few can surpass
> And thy fine nose, like purest diamond, could cut
>   glass.
> My love for thee cuts like a knife
> And gives passion to my life;
> For thee I would cut down all thy foes
> Who were not quelled by thy haughty nose.

The perfect curve of thy nose is unto a strung bow,
Piercing my breast with its flung arrow.

One other sonnet I wrote expressed my new spirituality, my ability to rise above pleasures of the mere flesh in order to serve Love's higher call, as well as metaphorically expressing the matching spirit Selina and I shared.

Now do I feel to pick my nose,
I fain would explore my flared nostrils,
This territory from which pleasure constantly flows
As hardened mucus from God's eternal mills.
Ah! What is so good as digging one's nose?
Nothing in the human sensation!
Yet, if my love to thy heart goes
Gladly would I abandon this daily meditation.
For the passion I feel for thee
Far surpasses even a nose-picking session;
I have dug deep of my nostrils and see
That true love hath a far better concession.
So I arise, ready to caress thy blushing cheek
My hands for thee freed, since boogers I no longer
    seek.

The reader will, I hope, understand the depth of my emotion and why I have only dared publish now I am well-established in life and love. Such raw emotion is not to be lightly displayed, and even now I worry that it may cause untold yearning in those who might not have a similar capacity for depth of feeling and, having read my verse, now wander through life forever unsatisfied, like men kissed by goddesses in dreams.

Another effect my great love had on me was to make me give up chocolate, or, at least, reduce my consumption. No one could have been more astonished at this effect than I. But I saw now that my love for chocolate had been a mere fancy, a boyish whim, in comparison to my burning passion for Selina.

Even before going to my *sanctum sanctorum* to write poetry, I distributed my stocks of Mars, Milky Ways, Cadburys, and so on to the neighbourhood children. (I did retain one packet of Smarties in case of emergencies. I was in love – *basodee*, as we say – not crazy.)

I passed a sleepless night. There was a great, raging energy in me which, had I been a lesser man, I would probably have expressed in some sort of physical activity. Instead, I wrote poetry, drank rum, thought deep thoughts, smoked several packets of cigarettes and planned my wedding. I think I dropped off to sleep only at around four in the morning.

The bedroom window of the apartment I was renting off campus had thin curtains, and so I awoke when the morning sun reached in and slapped me in the eyeballs. At least, that's what it felt like. Yet, curiously, after I splashed cold water on my face and with a careful fingernail removed the crust of *yampee* from my sleep-thickened eyelids, I found myself as fresh as a daisy. Of course, I had never actually seen a daisy, but I had heard they were the brightest things on mornings, along with the early birds out for a few worms.

I breakfasted lightly on a raw egg beaten up in a small glassful of rum with two aspirin. Despite my vigour, my head ached quite a bit. Writing poetry is no easy task, though I suppose the rum helped inspire me. In fact, that night proved to me that poetry writing should be classed among the high stress professions, right up there with police work, fire-fighting and dentistry. I now understood why it is that so many poets die early in life, although their life expectancy has reportedly improved since aspirin and swimming classes were invented.

I spent an hour or two polishing what I had written earlier that morning and marvelling, as all poets do, at the purity of my language and the power of my emotion. Of course, I knew even then that no one but Selina would ever see these immortal lines.

Such grand passion was not for the *macocious* eyes of an insensitive world. In fact, I decided I would not present my efforts to her until our wedding night.

I set off for campus at around 9 a.m. My leather briefcase was in hand and I was wearing my two-piece suit. (One of my keenest regrets from the previous day was that I had been dressed in a simple long-sleeved shirt and ordinary slacks. I could only hope that Selina looked beyond surface appearances and could see I was a man who, though forced into compromise with an opprobrious climate, was born to formal suits.)

I had two classes. Needless to say, I chafed as, in earlier years, had my thighs. But the gods of Love were with me because the first thing I saw as I entered the cafeteria at lunch-time was Selina having a midday cigarette. Not that she was a thing, of course: rather, a beauteous sight.

She was alone, reading. My heart beat like a trip-hammer as I went across, and sweat poured down my face. I was already perspiring pretty freely because even my two-piece suit tended to be rather confining. I took a moment to ply my handkerchief and then sat down.

'Hello, Selina,' I said. 'How are you?'

She looked up. Her face was like a white moon rising, and I thought I could write a poem about it. She was frowning a bit, then her face cleared.

'Ah!' she said. 'The T-shirt salesman.'

I was not surprised she remembered me. Clearly, we had both made strong impressions on each other.

Seeing that she was wearing the T-shirt she had purchased from me, I said, 'I see you're wearing the T-shirt you purchased from me.'

'Very good, Watson,' she said.

'Paras,' I corrected, a little put out that she should have forgotten my name.

'Is it comfortable?' I asked, knowing, as a woman, she would be touched by my solicitude. I am a fast worker once I get started.

'More comfortable than what you're wearing,' she said. 'Are you going to a wedding?'

'Not yet,' I said, understanding her hidden meaning at once.

'Oh,' she said. She looked back down at her book. Abashed at her openness, I thought.

'What are you reading?' I asked casually. I was just making conversation, and didn't even get the chance to brace myself for Selina's unexpected reply.

'*Macroeconomic Theory and Social Engineering*.'

I swallowed. She had spoken blithely, without a trace of embarrassment, and I realized this girl was spicier than hot pepper. For the first time, doubt assailed me: could I handle her?

'Interesting stuff?' I said, trying to sound carelessly bored.

'Very. I'm trying to get ready for a tutorial. I'm supposed to talk on "The effects of five-year plans on Caribbean societies".'

This was all coming a bit too fast for me. Had I been more experienced, I would doubtless have been blasé. As it was, I mopped my brow surreptitiously.

'I see,' I said. 'Well, I'm going to have some lunch.'

'You do that,' she said, not even looking up from her book.

I hesitate to use such strong language, but the fact was that this was a brazen display of intellect.

I left, realizing I had some serious thinking to do.

It might seem to the reader that, discovering Selina's casual display of intellect, a wise man would have backed off. Yet, as the old saying goes, who in love is not a fool? Or, to put it another way, who is wise in love? No man wants a woman who might be smarter than he, but I discovered I had a great capacity for love. There were in me unsuspected depths of passion. When I confess that I spent that entire day reading Greek drama and modern American literature, after recording the pitiless details of lunch in my diary, you will understand how deeply I was gripped.

Even so, I had no intentions of having an intellectual conversation with Selina. Such intimacy, I felt, was proper only between

41

man and wife. Although she had hinted that she had no inhibitions about using her mind, I felt I could show her a higher, finer world. Perhaps my love for her was only deepened by knowing I had to save her from herself. She was young yet, but if she continued on this path she might eventually become a socially conscious woman – perhaps even a feminist, though I did not think a woman of Selina's calibre could ever reach such a stage. But higher education has strange effects on the female psyche.

In order to protect her, however, I first had to get to know her.

This was not as easy a task as one might assume. Certainly, campus offered hundreds of opportunities for interaction. There were classes, study groups, various clubs – though only Jamaicans still used weapons to meet women – the Campus Bar and fêtes every weekend. But I did not want to meet her on the normal social round. I wanted a setting where she would see my hidden depths, shining like a star in the sky. To be sure, I had sold her a T-shirt and she had worn it. In some cultures – for example, the United States – that meant we were practically engaged. But I felt something more was needed.

I decided to have a tea party.

For someone else, such a function – or feat – might have been difficult to arrange. But I was a member of the Students' Guild. It was my first taste of the facility which power lends to romance. The Guild, you see, was a political organization. Thus, I was able to utilize its funds for a worthy end and justify it afterwards. The tea party was advertised as a fund-raising affair and I had the security of knowing that, if it failed to raise funds, no one expected it to do so anyway. After all, we were a political organization, not a profit-making one. (Indeed, if we *had* made money, students would have begun looking upon us with great suspicion.)

All Guild members, and those likely to ask leading questions, were given free tickets. The more persistent ones were promised hard-boiled eggs, which effectively silenced them. So there I was, well-organized.

42

A week before the scheduled affair, I sought out Selina and presented her with a ticket.

'How much?' she asked.

For a moment, I admit, I was tempted. But true love triumphed over my natural instinct to pocket hard cash.

'It's complimentary,' I said. 'Will you come?'

She shrugged. 'Sure. If I've nothing better to do.'

I went away, elated.

I put great effort into this tea party. I had the University Cantina order a few hundred tea bags, sugar, milk and several gallons of hot water. The tea party was to be held in the Guild Hall, and I made sure to book the Hall between 4.30 p.m. and 8.00 p.m., by which time I expected they would be dragging the bodies out. That having been done, I got into the real business of proper preparation.

You might wonder why I had chosen to have a tea party in order to impress Selina. The answer is obvious. Civilization owes many things to the British empire: the English language, cricket and steak-and-kidney pie. Yet the most civilized custom the Empire had bequeathed upon the natives was undoubtedly tea-drinking. Indeed, if Americans had adopted the custom of drinking tea, instead of dumping it in the Boston harbour, they might not today have a four trillion dollar debt and that informal breeziness of manner which gets them so disliked. In fact, I suspect that much of the social tension in the United States can undoubtedly be traced to their habit of drinking coffee in the morning instead of tea in the afternoon.

Be that as it may, I intended to take advantage of my country's historical legacy on that momentous afternoon. A lesser man would undoubtedly have treated the affair in a sanguine manner. A lesser man would have thought that, in the drinking of tea, all that is required is a hand with a reasonable number of fingers and the ability to inhale.

I knew better.

Tea-drinking, properly done, is as fine an art as wine-tasting.

Finer, since a wine-taster needs only sip and spit. A tea-drinker, like a ballerina, is born before being made. Just as the ballerina's foot must be shaped just so, so the true tea-drinker must have the right physical requirements. Tea, unlike wine, must be swallowed. So if one has an Adam's apple like a tennis ball, tea-drinking is not the best way to win a woman's affections. The most tolerant female, after all, may rightly baulk at the idea of seeing, for her entire married life, a throat which looks like a garden hose with a blocked nozzle.

In this respect, I had no worries. My Adam's apple was rounded, distinct without being noticeable. Yet even more important than this was the fact that I had a little finger. Actually, I had two, but, in the matter of drinking tea, only one mattered. As you know, it is impossible to drink tea in the Correct fashion without a little finger to extend. (The technical term, as I learned from my reading, is 'sticking out your pinky'.)

In drinking tea, the pinky is held perfectly perpendicular from the active hand and follows smoothly the pronation of the wrist as one tilts the cup. The handle of the teacup is, of course, held mainly with thumb and fore- and middle fingers. The third, or ring, finger serves mainly as a brace.

In order to attain perfection, training in the praying mantis style of kung fu is useful. So is playing golf.

I did not have these advantages but, through strenuous effort, I eventually was able to hold my cup properly. But there was more.

Tea, I learned, is never drunk. Instead, it must, in the deepest and truest sense of the word, be sipped. Without noise. This is not as easy as it seems. For hours I practised assiduously. I sipped cup after cup of tea. My bladder began to feel like a balloon, the kind they fly across France in. I stayed awake for three nights, learning that caffeine is a good substitute for sleep, though one does tend to jump at loud noises and cry for no reason at all. I was so full of tea I felt more like a vat than a human being.

It was only after the fourth day that I hit upon the secret. In the same way that I had perfected my BBC accent by eating green figs,

44

so did I employ another peculiarly British quality to drink tea properly – keeping a stiff upper lip. Not only did this enable me to drink my tea in perfect silence, but it automatically gave me that quintessentially British expression, as though one is smelling rotten fish. This is *so* crucial when one is drinking tea. The person who looks as if he is enjoying his tea is always suspected of drinking coffee.

Nobody takes this on in these lax modern times. I was determined, however, to adhere to the best standards of a bygone era. Selina, I knew, would expect nothing less than perfection from her chosen mate. I felt I could, with some effort, attain this.

The day for the tea party dawned bright and fair. At least, I assumed it did since when I awoke it was already riding high in the sky with a brightness which many people find offensive. Certainly, after four sleepless nights, when my only real pleasure had been emptying my bladder, I could have used something less luminous in the sky.

Be that as it may, I was looking forward greatly to the party. Here, I felt, was to be a turning-point in my life, a moment when I would display impeccably Correct behaviour to one who would truly appreciate it.

A turning-point it was. But not, alas, in the way I expected.

In retrospect, I do not think what happened at the tea party was really my fault. You must remember that I had just spent a hard week learning a skill it takes native Englishmen a lifetime to acquire. And they come from a society, unlike my own, where tea-drinking is considered essential to a good upbringing.

Had I not been a West Indian, I should surely have failed in my endeavour. However, the great strength of the societies of the English-speaking Caribbean has always been our ability to do English things better than the English themselves. We have produced writers who write better prose and better poetry than the English who first spoke the language. We have produced cricketers who play the game better than the English who invented it. And we have produced schoolteachers who whip children's bottoms far better than the English schoolmasters who first learned to enjoy it. (More on this in a later chapter.)

Arrogant as it might seem, therefore, I was confident that I would be able to drink tea just as well as the most English Englishman.

Nor, as I have just described, was I mistaken in my assumption. But the sheer effort of my efforts took it out of me. Having not slept for four nights, I finally entered the arms of Morpheus, as they used to say back in ancient Greece, for fourteen hours straight. This was on the night before the tea party. When I finally awoke, I felt dazed. I had a headache which passed only when I took a shot of rum. My mouth tasted like a week-old teabag and, looking at the clock, I saw that I was late. In fact, my intuition was perfectly accurate because, as I hurried to get ready, I felt a thread hanging out from between my lips and drew out the sodden bag from beneath my tongue. Throwing the bag in the bin, I brushed my teeth, gargled and took a bath. Luckily, deciding how I was going to dress had been the main issue on my mind for that tea-stimulated and sleepless week and my clothes had been laid out for three days now. This saved precious time.

I had already faced up to the fact that it was not within the sphere of practical politics to wear my three-piece suit for the entire afternoon. Being mostly a room where people read, smoked and threw bread, the Guild Hall was not air-conditioned. This limitation might have fazed, or even defeated, a lesser man. But, as I have pointed out, I was not a lesser man. I was determined to wear my full ensemble, as they say in France, for at least part of the festivities. Just let Selina see me in a three-piece suit *and* drinking tea, I felt, and the rest would be plain sailing.

In order for this to work, though, I would have to stand at the door, where there would be some cooling breezes. And that in turn meant I would have to both take tickets *and* look distinguished.

The reader will undoubtedly feel that in attempting this I was setting myself too stern a task. After all, there are men who can take tickets and men who can look distinguished. But could both be done at the same time? I did not know, but so great was my love for Selina that I was determined to try.

I dressed rapidly and reached the Hall exactly on time. The cantina staff had already laid out the materials and were ready to dispense the brew to the guests. My only worry was that the festivities might become too bacchanalian – tea, as I had discovered, could bite like an adder if consumed in sufficient quantities.

Nonetheless, as people started coming in, I concentrated on taking their tickets and looking polished. Sometimes, I ignored their stubs in my efforts to appear elegant and sometimes I took their tickets crudely and gracelessly. But, as the afternoon wore on, I managed to meld the two more easily.

Yet even this signal triumph failed to move me, for Selina had not yet appeared.

Women, I think, do not realize the trouble they cause by not being on time. Many thoughts went through my mind as, with increasing tension, I waited for Selina. Literature, I knew, was replete with examples of women's tardiness causing tragedy. If, for instance, Juliet had exercised just a little more care in her timing, Romeo would never have killed himself. Lack of time didn't allow Shakespeare to go more deeply into the matter, but it is likely that Juliet said to herself, 'Oh, I'll just take this potion and seem to be dead for a day or two. Romeo will be upset, but it won't be for long.' But exactly what women mean by 'long' is a question which has disturbed men since the beginning of measurement.

Even three centuries after Shakespeare, women's bad timing was still a major element in literature. Roderick Usher, you may recall, suffered severe trauma because Lady Madeline took so long to escape her grave.

Yet it is not only in fiction we find such examples of women's careless heed of time. History, too, is replete with carnage caused by women being late. I am convinced that the real reason

Napoleon failed to conquer Moscow was not because of the Russian winter but because his wife, Marie Louise, busy trying to get her make-up right, delayed his invasion. Sometimes, of course, feminine tardiness has good results. Hitler would have left that fateful bunker much earlier if Eva Braun hadn't taken so long to put on her leather underwear. In the Caribbean itself, I am sure Toussaint L'Ouverture managed to lead the first successful slave rebellion only because he didn't have a wife keeping him back saying, 'You mean you're going to your first rebellion dressed like *that*?'

And so I chafed impatiently as I stood at the door, wondering if another great tragedy was to be enacted because a woman was not on time.

That Selina might not come at all never occurred to me. I had great confidence in my own attractiveness, not having known many women. And besides, I remembered her words clearly and had written them down: 'Sure. If I've nothing better to do.' A girl like Selina, I felt, would not say 'sure' unless she meant it. And what better *could* she have to do?

At 6:02 my faith was justified and she appeared in the dusk. She seemed like a fair goddess as she moved through the fading light, dressed in a white cotton top with a round neck and puffed sleeves and – I blinked, scarcely able to credit my senses – denim jeans.

I reeled and, had my trousers not been so well starched, would surely have fallen. That Selina, a girl with a British mother, would come to a tea party in jeans was something I could scarcely believe.

Yet, after the first shock, my next emotion was, strangely enough, one of overwhelming tenderness. All at once, I could see the situation as clearly as if it had been a movie. The young girl, born to parents of different background. Her British mother, torn away from her homeland to come and live in an underdeveloped Caribbean island. Probably pining away, neglecting to instruct her growing daughter in the important matters of life. And what was the result? Selina, to all appearances unaware of anything amiss, shows up at a Guild tea party in jeans.

Jean Rhys, you will remember, dealt with a similar situation in *Wide Sargasso Sea*. And, like Antoinette Cosway, I realized that Selina was a girl who needed the love and guidance of a well-dressed man.

Tenderness or not, though, I had to make a quick decision. To my fevered mind, I could already see the surreptitious glances, hear the mocking whispers. Should I risk my social position by greeting Selina? It was a moment for instant decisions. Fortunately, Selina had stopped to exchange a few words with an acquaintance. In less than five minutes, my tempestuous passions won out over the call of social norms. I went forward to meet her!

I would not, in all honesty, term this an act of raw courage. The fact was, I was in the grip of emotions I was scarcely able to control. There was something about Selina – her aristocratic nose, her large calves, her pale skin – which seemed to stir the depths of my soul. Add to this her wanton display of intelligence and her perfect pronunciation, and she became an irresistible soup. I wanted nothing more than to be her spoon!

'Hello,' I said.

She turned to me, her face like a pale flower in the gathering night.

'Hi,' she said.

She turned back to her acquaintance – a young man dressed in a T-shirt and jeans with a knapsack slung on his back. It was an interesting aspect of Selina, I thought, that despite her clear superiority, she spoke to all sorts of people.

'Check you later, nah,' she said, in a perfect Trinidadian accent.

I almost gasped. Were there no boundaries this girl didn't cross?

The fellow walked off and Selina started walking towards the Hall. I had to trot a bit to keep up.

'How are you?' I asked.

'Fine. And yourself?'

'Quite well,' I replied.

The conversation, I thought, was already moving along nicely. Encouraged, I said, 'Would you care to join me for a cup of tea?'

She shrugged. 'All right.'

We went over to one of the small round tables, which was covered with a white cloth. I pulled out a chair and Selina sat. I then took off my jacket, pausing for a few additional moments so she would have time truly to appreciate the elegance and dignity of my appearance, and draped it over the back of my chair.

After a moment's hesitation, I pulled my chair over so I would be sitting next to rather than opposite her. A forward gesture, I know, but as I have said I was in the grip of a passion stronger than myself. Indeed, I didn't even feel significantly relieved that we were sitting and that no one could see Selina had jeans on unless they were right next to us. Proper dress no longer seemed to matter.

Alas, I was to find out all too soon how proper wear *always* matters.

The tea came. I raised my steaming cup to Selina. 'To civilized evenings and pleasant conversation,' I said.

She looked at me with bright eyes and the corner of her mouth twitched briefly. I think she was trying not to reveal how impressed she was at my hidden depths. Although, given my suit, she ought not to have been surprised.

Within the next minute, though, I found out why my suit had not given Selina the image of sophistication I had hoped for.

I took a sip of my tea. Although I did it casually, I was straining every sinew and concentrating fiercely in order to ensure that I performed the ritual properly. My pinky was out, my wrist firm as I tipped the cup at an exact forty-five degree angle. I sipped – no sound. Selina was looking at me intently.

'Are you all right?' she asked.

'Of course,' I said.

'No diarrhoea or anything like that?'

'No,' I answered, adding politely, 'but thank you for inquiring.' I realized she could not know my great love for her had put me off chocolate. I was even farting less.

The tea was not sweet enough. There was no sugar on the table, and I rose to signal the waitress. As I sat down, Selina said, 'You missed two loops in your belt.'

She said this quite casually, so that for a few seconds the full import of her words did not impact on my mind.

'Excuse me?' I stammered, certain I had heard wrong.

'You missed two loops. In the back of your trousers,' she said, still in the same conversational way.

'Ah,' I said.

Very casually, I reached behind me and ran my finger along my belt. Sure enough, in my hurry to dress, I had run my belt over, instead of through, the double loop at the back of my trousers. Fortunately, my jacket had hidden my gaffe till then. I felt the hot blush of shame mantle my cheek.

'Excuse me for a moment,' I said.

I stood up and simultaneously slipped on my jacket. I did it so smoothly I am confident no one even saw that my belt was crooked. But, of course, the one person who mattered already knew.

I went quickly to the gents' room and adjusted my belt. Then I returned to the hall, putting what I hoped was a carefree smile on my face.

'All fixed,' I told Selina.

She nodded. I could not tell what was passing through her mind. But I realized I had lost ground. What woman would have faith in a man who could not be trusted to loop his belt properly? She might be thinking a loose belt signified a loose character. She might even be thinking that I was the sort of man who let his trousers drop at a moment's notice. I shuddered inside at the image thus brought up.

Intent on changing whatever impression she might have formed in this regard, I crossed my left leg over my right leg in order to display my trousers' knife-edge crease. Such a crease, I felt, would show I was a man who would not casually crumple my trousers by letting them drop. (I could, of course, have invited her home to see my closet, where my trousers were all in special hangers

51

clipped by the folds at the end of the legs. But it was too early in our relationship for that.)

'How is your tea?' I asked.

She took a sip. 'Fine.'

She glanced down at my crossed legs.

'You must have dressed quite hurriedly,' she said.

A nameless fear coiled through my stomach.

'Why do you say that?'

'You have two different socks on.'

In utter disbelief, I looked down at the length of sock exposed by my risen trouser fold. Sure enough, although both my socks were blue, one was navy blue and the other – even now, so many years later, I wince at the memory – was royal blue.

It was the end. Even the unmarried Toussaint would have reeled under a blow like this. I drained my cup in a single gulp, and in doing so pronated my wrist far too much. But I no longer cared. My great love had been clubbed down before it had even got started, and I no longer cared about anything.

I stood up. 'Thank you for a lovely evening,' I told Selina, and walked out of her life forever.

Chapter Four

This was his logic, and his arm so strong,
His cause prevailed, and he was never wrong.

From 'School Champion' by
George Crabbe

Now that I am in my more mature years, I realize I might have handled the situation with Selina differently. If it happened now – not that I have ever worn mismatched socks since that fateful day – I would have tried to convince her that my socks were, in fact, alike.

A bold ploy, you say. Yet I know now that in order to be successful with women one needs to be bold. This, and not his Americanism, was the real secret of North's attractiveness to the opposite sex. I distinctly remember him once showing up for a university fête, dressed in jeans and track shoes. He was accompanied by a quite pretty woman and his girlfriend, who he thought was studying that night but who had changed her mind and come to the fête, was naturally quite upset.

'But everybody in America goes to parties in jeans and track shoes,' North told her.

It was, of course, an absurd argument. Despite their Cuban policy, even Americans could not have so casual a dress code. Yet within five minutes – I do not exaggerate – North had his girlfriend convinced he was properly dressed. As for the woman on his arm, he told his girlfriend she was his cousin.

It was this incident which convinced me that North's American-ism was the way to go. In the following year, I began speaking from the back of my mouth. I never quite lost the pronunciation I had practised so assiduously from the BBC, but it was not long before people asked me regularly if I had lived in the US or if I was practising to be a radio DJ. This was to stand me in good stead in later life.

I should emphasize, however, that it was not with any intentions of romantic or even financial success that I strove to improve my accent. After that Evening of Shame, as I like to call it, love was turned to ashes in my bosom. I could not face Selina again, and when I passed her on campus I merely smiled politely and nodded, wearing the mask.

I realized, though, I would have to face the world some day. And so I plunged myself into my studies. Cultivating an American accent was merely part of my programme of self-improvement. It may seem strange to the reader that, given my natural advantages, I should have been so concerned about improving myself. After all, I had only to use peroxide on my hair, and my status in society would be virtually guaranteed. But I have always believed in fully exploring one's potential. Except for deference and a high-paying job, I didn't want only the things I could get because my skin was fair.

But there were many people to whom such attributes meant little or nothing, though fortunately they had no influence in society. I was determined that even those persons should respect me. Ambition, and a desire to meet impossible challenges, was part of my unusual character. Yet it was my failure with Selina which had brought out this fire in me.

That I reacted in this manner was not entirely surprising. I had not until then failed at anything in life – this was the advantage of a sheltered upbringing where one never had to do anything.

Now, however, the very foundations of my world had been shattered. Despite my impeccable speech, I was as other men – I put on my pants one leg at a time and didn't belt them properly. And I had discovered that having several pairs of socks, far from providing security and a sense of worth, created confusion in a world where a moment's inattention could mean disaster.

Now my heart was not merely broken; it was shattered into a thousand pieces. There was nothing left but to lose myself in academia.

And yet it was in work that I found my true self. Truly God moves in mysterious ways and sometimes, according to my visions, in a convertible.

On the fourth floor of the University Library, there was an area called the Caribbean Section. I had not had cause to use it before, having been satisfied with copying my notes out of the reference books in the General Section and then transferring them into my essays and papers. By this tried and true method, I had so far managed to maintain a steady B average, sometimes doing a little better when I was lucky enough to find an article written by the lecturer for the subject. Quoting lecturers back at themselves always guaranteed a few extra marks, even if my topic was 'The impact of emancipation on women's liberation and sexual positions' and the lecturer's article dealt with 'West Indian pathos and rum in Sam Selvon'. A little adaptation, a few leaps in logic, and one easily reaped the benefits of people liking to hear themselves.

I was doing a paper entitled 'The black Jacobins – the first minstrels?' and I knew C.L.R. James had written a book on the Jacobins. The only copies were in the Caribbean Section so I went up to take some notes. The book itself proved useless – the Jacobins apparently didn't even have a barber-shop quartet – but there was a photograph of Mr James in the frontispiece of the book. To my utter surprise, James was a black man. Naturally, I had assumed that anyone with three initials before his last name was white. But this discovery, like a bright light bursting in my head, showed me otherwise.

A rapid perusal of other volumes with author photographs in the Caribbean Section revealed that many – indeed the vast majority – of academics and writers there were black. And, like a glorious vision, new vistas opened up before me.

For the first time, I began to consider seriously pursuing writing as my career.

After all, as I now knew, other people from the Caribbean had done it. Admittedly, all of them lived in the temperate and developed countries – Britain or the United States. But why could I not also become a writer? I could already speak in both accents, and it should be easy enough to get a fur coat. As for becoming developed, I was halfway there already.

There was something attractive in the idea of writing as a career. I would be enriching the culture of my country, shaping the way people thought and demonstrating to the world that we were capable of intellectual effort.

Of course, I had no intention of pursuing such a career unless there was money in it. If I couldn't write, I would take up fashion designing. But I figured there had to be money in literature: rents in Britain and the United States were fearfully high. Of course, I realized that the low overhead probably helped keep the writers' profit margins wide, too – authors generally needed nothing but a typewriter, paper and some addictive drug. Some of them were even vegetarian, though I could not conceive reaching this awful extreme.

But there were other, more abstract reasons why I had this desire to be a writer. For one thing, I would be able to smoke a pipe. This, I was sure, would have the women clustering around me, to coin a simile, like bees to honey. For sheer sophistication, you can't beat a pipe. But, of course, you need to be an author or a professor or a scientist in order to carry it off. Otherwise you just look silly. Even Wall Street financiers and dictators of Third World countries can't smoke pipes to good effect, since everyone expects to see them in cigars.

There were other advantages. No matter what kind of writing I was doing, it would enable me to sit and stare into space for long hours and get paid for it. In fact, one of the things which convinced me that I was meant to be a writer was that I was already in the habit of doing this.

I had every confidence I could become a successful writer. After all, I was already better than most of the past ones. C.L.R. had been a womanizer. Jean Rhys – artist's model, mannequin and occasional prostitute – was almost exactly his opposite number, an outright manizer.

If people of such loose morals could be successful writers, I figured my moral superiority would obviously enable me to write far better than they. I could, I felt, model myself after Shakespeare, the Bible and Ernest Hemingway. Already my writing, like Hemingway's, was quite simple in style. Indeed, I rarely used words of more than two syllables. And it would take little effort, I felt, to become as one critic had described him, 'a fat drunk'. Remember, too, I was already writing what was, in my opinion, extraordinary poetry. Far better than Derek Walcott's stuff, which, believe it or not, didn't always rhyme and dealt with issues like nearly burning off his balls with some white powder. I mean, who really wants to read sports poetry in these grim times?

I must admit, though, that when I tried it, writing proved to be far more difficult than I had anticipated. Over the next five weeks, I wrote my first short story. The initial steps were relatively easy. I opened my thesaurus, my dictionary and a case of rum. I grew my hair long in the back and, to round off my literary image, bought a pair of eyeglasses and a raspberry beret. Then I sat down to think, and this is where I ran into trouble.

It wasn't that my spelling and grammar needed work. (I mean, they did, but that's what publishing houses hire proofreaders for and I, for one, would be the last to deny a man an honest day's work.) But I discovered a short story needs a plot, characters, dialogue and other such troublesome things. I must have cleaned out my pipe and tamped in fresh tobacco about ten times before I finally began. (A brief word of advice to aspiring young writers: leave the windows of your room open while working – this prevents the smoke from gathering and allows a fast exit in case of a carelessly thrown match.)

The short story I eventually wrote might, on a cursory examination, be considered immature. But critics of greater depth will understand that what I was attempting to do was capture the innocence of childhood and the confusion of approaching maturity. It was, I suppose, the process I myself was undergoing at the time I wrote it. I also wrote in a manner which I hoped would be accessible to even the most unsophisticated reader. Looking back on it now, I have no hesitation in describing this as one of the great West Indian short stories. I call it 'Adolescence's Dream':

See Dick and Jane. They are on Maracas Beach. Dick is in a blue swim trunks. Jane is in a green bikini. Her breasts are now starting to bud. Dick goes into the sea. The waves are strong.

'Come on in, Jane,' he shouts. 'The water's fine!'

Jane wades into the water.

'Oh, it is cold,' she says.

'Come all the way in,' says Dick, 'then you won't feel it.'

Is Dick being Freudian? He watches how Jane's nipples harden in the cold and he feels it. He wonders: does Jane want to feel it?

Jane comes into the water. She hugs Dick.

'Oh, I am so cold,' she says.

'I wouldn't mind warming you up, lady,' says Dick, in a flash of maturity. He presses her to him, like a heater on a wrinkled shirt. The waves crash around them.

'Oh, Dick,' says Jane. She sounds breathless.

'Yes, I have one,' says Dick, realizing it for the first time.

They look at each other, knowing their life has changed forever. But they know also that, if they trust in God, they will be all right.

The story, as I say, took me five weeks to write. I managed to emulate Hemingway while adding the moral pointer which his writing sorely lacked. Few, if any, Caribbean writers have ever captured the sadness and passion of youth as well as I have in this story. Only Michael Anthony, perhaps, has come close; Wilson Harris was deep but, as one critic pointed out, it was inadvisable to operate heavy machinery while reading his prose.

Encouraged by my first attempt at writing, I looked around for guidance from other, more established writers. To tell the truth, I didn't expect to find any living Caribbean writers. Imagine my delight, therefore, when I discovered one who was not only alive but living in Trinidad and working right on campus. His name was a well-respected and venerable one: White. Charlie P.T. White, better known to the public as 'Brain'. Little did I know, when I went to search him out, how ill-fated our literary relationship was to be.

The granting of sobriquets is a common custom in Trinidad. 'Brain' White had been given his nickname by those who found his head resembled a pumpkin. Admittedly, there was another school of thought which argued that his head bore a closer relationship to a water melon. Both sides acknowledged, however, that there were few larger heads to be found on the island and agreed that a head of that size had to have something in it.

The writing career of Brain bore out this assumption. Twenty-two years before the time I got to know him, Brain had joined that very select class of persons who have had a letter to the editor published. At that time, he was twenty-six years old – quite young to have his work published. The letter – on the topic of tropical weather and deathly irony – enjoyed moderate success, bringing forth two responses.

A year later, Brain managed to have another letter, a poem, published in the papers. It was a signal triumph in a society which does not read poetry and, the following year, he published at his own cost a slim volume of poetry and prose. It was this that I discovered in the University Library. When I tell you that said volume was bound in limp, mauve leather, you will understand the sensitivity and passion he brought to his Art. Indeed, I was later to see him sit for two hours looking at a cockroach while he composed an 'Ode to the Eternal Insect'.

Since this first – in fact, only – publication, Brain had managed to hold down a series of writing jobs. Indeed, such was the power of his intellect that he held the Caribbean record for getting the widest literary reputation out of one book and his hundreds of pamphlets – no easy feat in a society where slim volumes of verse were as common as leaves in the wind. (At the time I met him, however, this record was being seriously challenged by columnist Merle Shoelace who, as you know, wrote the column 'The dancer can't drag on' – a moving piece about a dancer who has to run a rickshaw in order to get money for ballet shoes – and several others in the Sunday newspaper. But more on her later.)

I thought long and carefully before approaching Brain. I knew he might not have much time for an aspiring writer, and so I prepared thoroughly in order to convince him I was worth his time and attention.

First, I studied his poetry, which I knew to be excellent because I didn't understand a word of it. Then I wrote a letter to the editor, modelled carefully on Brain's style. I figured the same principle which worked for lecturers should work for Brain, who worked in the University Printery.

Although I had intended to do so only as an exercise, the resulting letter was so well-written I decided to actually send it off to the editor. It was an impulsive decision, I admit, and perhaps even a bold-faced one. Yet it taught me a valuable lesson: to wit, one makes no progress in this world without a modicum of bold-facedness.

My letter was never published. But the editor did send me a kind note, advising me that my style had potential and I should keep trying. This encouraged me greatly, and perhaps the reader might find it interesting to read the letter which, in a sense, launched my public career.

> The Editor:
>
> I would like to use your medium, by your gracious permission, to inform the Minister of Utilities that there is a leaking tap at #7 Wares Road which has been leaking for two weeks now. The dry season will be here next month – September – and this problem should be attended to before residents face a serious water shortage.
>
> Public Observer.

Not the best letter ever penned, I admit. Yet there was a certain precision and informed tone to it which boded well for my later careers in both the media and politics and, of course, as Paras P. In fact, fifteen years later, when I entered parliament, the first thing I did was approach the then Minister of Public Works and draw his attention to the selfsame leak. The matter was attended to in the same week.

The letter, including research, took me two weeks to write. I spent the following month writing another, more ambitious epistle. On the night of the day I sent it off, I had a strange dream.

I had gone to bed as usual in my apartment at around 10 o'clock. (With the pressure of study and trying to lay the foundation of a writing career, I kept quite late hours.) The next morning, I thought my dream had its genesis in the five *bara*, two soak pommecythere and several pieces of *anchar* with a small bowl of ice cream for dessert I had before hitting the bed. But I later realized I had a paranormal experience – although it occurs to me now that it is possible eating five *bara*, two soak pommecythere and several pieces of *anchar* with a small bowl of ice cream for dessert may well *contribute* to a paranormal experience. Perhaps the Society of Parapsychology, in conjunction with Weight Watchers, could investigate. I only suggest.

But I was telling you about my dream.

61

It was very vivid, like yellow socks. I saw and heard as though I was in real life – in fact, rather better since, like so many men of powerful intellect, I rarely paid attention to what was around me in real life.

I dreamed I was in a large room with a huge metal machine. The machine had giant hair curlers on it, and I remember thinking, why would anyone with perfectly straight hair want to curl it? In fact the rollers were not curling hair, but sending out leaves of paper. I realized then that the machine was a printing-press.

Seated at the far end of the press, stacking paper, was a figure with a most enormous head. He looked around as I approached and then stood up. Despite the size of his head – or, according to Mr Einstein's theory of relativity, perhaps because of it – his body was quite small. He was so knock-kneed he could have replaced the castanet player in a Spanish band just by walking fast. He seemed surrounded by a halo of light.

Then he spoke, and his voice echoed sonorously in my head, like the tones of some gigantic and wonderful bell.

'Son of Morning, hast thou come to carry on my great task?'

When I answered, it was in the voice of the child I had not been for so many years. Even in my dream, I cringed with embarrassment.

'Me ain't know no Mr Morning. My name is Parmanandansingh.'

His burning gaze fastened upon me.

'Is it to thee my Holy Grail is to be passed?' he asked.

A glimmer of understanding came through the fog of my mind.

'Well, I could sew up your grail if it don't have too much hole. I doing sewing in the university.'

He opened his arms and some pamphlets fell out of his armpits. The light grew more intense and, suddenly, I awoke. For a full minute I lay gasping for breath. It may have been my asthma, but I think not. For, although I tried to dismiss the dream as just a fancy, when I got up and looked in the mirror I saw something which confirmed that what I had experienced had been no ordinary dream. How else could you explain the fact that in my dream I had been blushing with shame at speaking in the untutored accents of my childhood, and when I looked in the mirror *I found my cheeks still suffused with blood*!

I stayed at home that day, thinking deeply. And, if any vestiges of doubt still remained in my mind, they vanished like airplanes over the Bermuda triangle when I opened the papers the next day and saw my letter on the editorial page!

Mark, dear reader, the utter strangeness of this. I had posted my letter barely two days ago. Surely not enough time for the mail to be picked up, be delivered to the newspaper's offices, and then to be published. Oh, conceivably, it *could* have happened. Assuming great efficiency on the part of the postal service. But was that not in itself a sign of Divine Intervention?

When you consider, in addition to all the other evidence, the content of my first published work, the answer becomes obvious.

The Editor:
    Economic woes have been bedevilling our nation for a long time now. What is the solution? All around us we see people complaining that they do not have enough money, or work, or prosperity. But they complain because their priorities are wrong. Faith in the Lord is sufficient to all things thereof. Look at our priests in the Roman and Anglican Churches, even our pastors in the smaller churches, even our pundits with their large bellies? God is a generous God who provides amply for all His servants. So stop complaining and start praying! A nation of the faithful is a prosperous one and 'shall flourish like a green bay tree'.
                            Religious Public Observer.

That same day, I gathered up my stories, articles and poetry and went to meet Charlie P.T. White. According to my diary, I wore my blue three-piece suit with a dark grey tie, green shirt, black socks and grey shoes. Perfectly appropriate for such an important occasion.

The press was clanking noisily when I arrived and there was no sign of the man I had come to meet. I inquired of a wizened janitor where I might find Mr White and he gestured to a small wooden office at the far end of the room. I walked across and entered.

Brain looked exactly as he had in my dream, except he was eating a ham sandwich and reading one of his own pamphlets. Remember, I had never seen this man before, except in the black-and-white photograph adorning the front cover of his slim volume of poetry and prose. Yet I had dreamed him! Amazement held me dumb for a few seconds, though I felt perfectly natural. Perhaps it was because he was the first real writer I had ever met and so I felt no need for the spoken word.

He looked up from his pamphlet, still chewing. It was one of the first things that struck me – the versatility of the man. On the few occasions I had tried to read and eat at the same time, I had ended up with either a headache or stomach trouble. On one memorable occasion, when Prince Albert visited Trinidad, I had eaten pot roast and boiled cabbage while reading Jane Austen's *Emma*, and got dyspepsia along with a migraine. (Jane Austen, I am told, often has this effect on readers, even without the boiled cabbage.)

'Can I help you?' said White.

He was in his early forties. His voice was a deep and resonant bass. He sounded a bit irritated, as any man would be if interrupted while reading an important pamphlet.

'Sorry to bother you . . .' I began.

'Pause for just a trifle of time,' he said.

He put down the pamphlet and finished the sandwich in three huge bites. This was the next thing I noticed about Brain White – his impeccable manners. Although I was a perfect stranger, he did not keep me waiting and, as soon as he had finished his sandwich, he wiped his mouth with the back of his hand so as to save time.

He stood up, running his thick fingers through his long black locks. You could tell he was a writer just by his hair, and he wore spectacles. Yet he was very tall and had a large stomach. When he moved out from behind the desk, I saw the final proof of my vision: his knees were so knocked I immediately felt a sympathetic ache in my own testicles.

'You have material you would like to have printed?' he asked, seeing the folder in my hand. 'Five dollars a page, including the typesetting. Twenty dollars for binding, not including labour. Professional job guaranteed.'

'Uh, yes,' I said. After all, I couldn't say no after he had quoted his advertisement at me for free. It would not have been Correct. Besides, it seemed a good way to bring in the rather sensitive subject of my writing.

'What are the chronological parameters of the task?'

'Eh?'

'How soon you want it?'

'Oh, any time,' I said.

He turned to a ledger on his desk and ran a finger down one page. 'I think that time frame will prove eminently suitable,' he said.

He held out a hand for the folder and, feeling as though I was reaching out to Fate, I handed it over.

Quite naturally, he opened the folder to look through the material. When he came to the clipping of my published letter, he stiffened slightly and his sharp gaze stabbed at me.

'You are a worshipper of the Muse?' he said.

I smiled diffidently, not wanting to get into a religious debate. Brain seemed to take this as an affirmative.

'How long have you been a student of the moving pen?' he asked.

'Well, I'm in the Arts faculty,' I answered, 'but I'm not doing that course yet. I want to be a writer, though.'

'Of course. Who among us does not?' asked Brain.

Offhand, I could think of quite a few. But I supposed Brain

65

moved in more artistic circles. I waited while he read through my
letter to the editor.

After a period which seemed like a million years, but which in
truth could not have been more than 78 seconds – I timed him by
my watch and wrote it down later – he said, 'I see a certain
potential, a certain rough promise, in this epistle.'

I felt as if bells were chiming in my head. This was partly
because the university clock was striking the hour outside, but it
was also because of the feeling of deep contentment which rose
within me, like the gas you get at the dentist.

'Rest your weary bones and let us have a meeting of minds,'
said Charlie P.T. 'Brain' White; and so our ill-fated relationship
commenced.

He insisted I call him Brain. I would not have in the normal way
since, as is so often the case when one calls somebody after an
organ, I always felt I was mouthing an obscenity. Later, I was glad
of this.

'So you want to become a disciple of the Muse, eh?' he said.

'Yes,' I answered.

'It is not an easy thing,' he said. 'It is not just a matter of picking
up a pen and starting to write.'

I nodded.

'Being a writer requires this.' He pointed at his head, as if such
a head would need attention drawn to it. 'And this,' he added,
pointing to his upper torso.

'A plaid shirt?' I asked, puzzled.

'Heart, my boy, heart.'

'Oh, heart.'

He clasped his hands in front of him and, noticing a crumb of
bread which had fallen off his ham sandwich, picked it up between
two thick fingers and ate it.

'One can be a certified genius – the type of man who knows
how to spell "intransigent". One can be a new Chomsky and
make one's subject agree with one's verb nine times out of ten.
One might even be the kind of person who understands what James

66

Brown is singing. But,' he tapped the table with each word for emphasis, 'one won't be a writer.'

He grasped his shirt front passionately. 'To be a writer takes this.'

I frowned. 'Pockets?'

'Heart, my boy, heart.'

Brain steepled his fingers. 'It is heart which keeps you struggling on when everybody else is falling by the wayside, wearied by spelling. It is heart which keeps you striving heroically when others are giving up, bludgeoned by syntax. It is heart which keeps you searching for that Holy Grail – is something amiss?'

'No,' I said, having just jumped at his use of this phrase from my dream. Of course, now I was awake I knew the Holy Grail was not a shirt brand. Brain used the term as a metaphor; unless he was talking about some kind of colander.

'The Holy Grail,' he continued, 'of the Perfect Word.'

Obviously, it was a metaphor. Probably from one of those classic books. Not for the first time, I regretted the shortsightedness of those who made up the literature courses.

Brain said, 'In order to even begin to be a writer, you need this.'

He grasped the pocket of his shirt and, quick as a whip, I said, 'Heart?'

'Well, yes,' he said, pulling out a ballpoint pen from the pocket. 'But you also need this.'

'A Bic?' I asked.

'Of course. Smooth flow, convenient size, and quite cheap. I sell them. Dollar for one.'

I bought five Bic pens, to show him how serious I was about writing. A less committed man would undoubtedly have bought just two, and called it good.

'I can tell you're a man who possesses heart in full measure,' said Brain, smiling.

I was pleased to know this, but there were even graver matters pertaining to writing which I needed to know about. There were

67

so many questions bubbling within me, but I asked the obvious one first.

'Do you make any money out of writing?

'A writer cannot be overly concerned with financial renumeration,' said Brain, a little irritatedly, flicking out a hairy wrist with a thick gold ID band on it. He must have noticed my disappointed expression because he continued in a more kindly tone. 'But if you're willing to work hard and have a sturdy pair of shoes, you can get sponsorship from corporations for your writings. If you're persistent and sincere – and of course talented – you can get them to give you substantial sums just to get you off their backs. And you don't even have to account for how you spend the money.'

'You don't?' I said, doubtfully.

'Art cannot be controlled or dictated to,' Brain explained.

'It sounds like an idyllic existence,' I said enviously.

'The women can be a problem, though,' said Brain.

My eyes widened. 'Women?' I said.

He nodded. 'Women find intellectual men irresistible. They either worship me or fall deeply in love with me. I don't know which is worse. But I try to do what I can to bring a little cheer into their otherwise drab and meaningless existence. There are many women whom I have told to have sex with me if they want to improve their lives.' He sighed. 'I do what I can, but they know I am committed to my Muse. Like Atlas, I carry the world on my shoulders.'

I nodded understandingly. Drawing all those maps, I thought at the time, must have been a terrific strain. Later, though, I found out that Brain had never actually written any geography books.

'And, then, of course, one has to deal with the social burden of living a life devoted to Literature,' he continued.

'You mean being isolated from the common activities of humankind – observing life instead of living it?' I asked. We had been doing Huxley in class just that week.

'No, I mean being asked to make speeches at weddings all the time. It is a great honour, of course, and one likes to please the

68

fans. But it is not easy proposing not to detain people long on this joyous occasion. I've had to start charging a small fee for my services. After all, you don't expect the priest to perform for free.'

'Unless small boys are around,' I said absently.

'What?'

'Nothing,' I said, realizing that Brain, being the type of man who provided service both to women and weddings, probably saw himself as a sort of priest.

'I also have a regular classified ad so people can write to me and receive writing lessons. I charge a minimal fee – just enough to cover costs and keep me in cigarettes and beer, and pay for a good movie now and then. Have you seen *Deadly Revenge of the Seven Ninjas?*'

I shook my head, realizing how uncultured I must seem to this urbane and sophisticated man.

'Why don't you attend a cinematic perfomance with my wife and I tomorrow night?'

'Really?' I said.

'Of course.'

I stammered out my thanks and left. I could hardly wait for the hours to pass.

Brain's wife was not at all what I expected. Although she was white – I suppose Brain felt some ancestral sense of *noblesse oblige* for his name – she did not impress me as a woman of intellectual refinement. She seemed to be all hair and teeth. The man who ran his fingers through her hair would have been well advised to mark a trail, so that they could find their way back.

You also had to look very carefully to make sure she had eyes under that thick fringe, which we call a 'donkey maid', and when you did find them you felt that somewhere there was a necklace missing a pair of beads. Her eyes had that penetrating quality which looks straight through a man and right into his bank balance.

Her name was Gwendolyn. With a Y. I should have been warned.

Despite my fervent admiration of him, I did not expect perfection of Brain. If he liked a woman with teeth that could have built some pretty good dams and who spoke like she had a hot potato in her mouth, that was his prerogative. But it made me wonder.

At least I understood why Brain horned her so frequently. At first I thought he was just a passionate debauchee, although at his age I suppose it would have been more accurate to call him a dirty old man. But, although I am sure he truly loved her, the need to sleep with a woman with fewer incisors must, despite Brain's strength of will, have been intense.

As I was to soon discover, though, the matter went far deeper than that. But, since Gwendolyn wore a long-sleeved top and slacks that night, I had no inkling of the truth. In fact, her fashion sense was not at all bad.

For this reason, I ignored my reservations and treated her as one of my own class and complexion. At least, in the latter respect, I had no cause to dissemble. Gwendolyn was Canadian, and Canadians are some of the whitest people on earth.

The film we attended was a double feature: *Deadly Revenge of the Seven Ninjas* and *Ninja Robot vs Godzilla*. However, the second film was just commercial trash and we left in disgust.

Brain, who was driving, said, 'It is a measure of the shallowness of thought that a cinema owner would see fit to show two such entirely different films just because of a superficial similarity in the titles. Couldn't they see that the subject matter, the themes, the very heart of the two films were entirely different? Have we so lost the ability to distinguish between uplifting Art and degenerate Mammon?'

I hadn't noticed the names of the directors, but it was obvious Brain didn't like this Mammon's work one bit.

'Not everyone is as perceptive as you, darling,' said Gwendolyn.

'But it was perfectly clear,' Brain said. '*Deadly Revenge of the Seven Ninjas* deals with one of the fundamental drives of human nature. Seven, as you know, represents perfect social unity while the ninja's invisibility represents the power of the overlooked to destroy the obvious and powerful. Ralph Ellison's *Invisible Man* dealt with the same theme.'

I drew in my breath sharply. It was such a joy to be in contact, not only with a man of such powerful intellect, but one who could see the deeper meaning in everything.

Brain's ability to find meaning in everything was not merely confined to art. As our acquaintance ripened, I heard him discourse on topics as varied as chalk and cheese. (The reason white chalk was used on blackboards to teach children, he said, was a subtle way of imposing colour status values upon impressionable minds. Cheese, on the other hand, represented the gradual evolution of the world economy from white Western values to yellow Asian standards.)

I was even there when he prepared his well-known pamphlet *Amoebic Dysentery – Implications for Our Nation*. This pamphlet, as well as any other, reflects the breadth of Brain's vision. But I remember it particularly because many of the points he raised in it had been discussed by the two of us the night before. It was characteristic of the man that he never gave me credit for it – not that I wanted any.

However, I did save the working notes, draft and final published versions. Here, then, are the parts of that well-known pamphlet I consider myself directly responsible for. Brain, I admit, had a deeper historical and social understanding of dysentery than I at this time. (But, remember, I was still quite young then.) So, while the style is unmistakably Brain's, it was my dictionary we used.

> Thanks to the putative indifference of the slothful
> bureaucrats at the Health Ministry, the Nation has found
> itself in the dire situation where persons with weak, even
> ulceric stomachs are at gut-wrenching risk each time they
> perambulate to the toilet, and even more at risk when they
> leave that haven which, if smelly, is at least safe.

Feminism must accept at least partial responsibility for something being foul in the state of Denmark. Before the advent of the fanatic-eyed bra-burners, women were interested only in the burners on their stoves. Their husbands and children had home-cooked meals.

Feminism changed this by helping create fast-food places. As modernist women began to abandon their traditional domestic duties in order to do real work, men either had to cook or starve. Feminism also led to more bachelors in the population, since women suddenly wanted to be treated like human beings – a phenomenon which had never before happened in recorded history and which probably does much to explain the parlous and chaotic state of 20th-century society.

Fortunately, a compromise was reached and Colonel Sanders and Ronald Mcdonald became millionaires by hiring women to cook for them and by selling their nutritious products to the millions of men thrown on the bread loaf. Civilization was saved by these heroic men – but we must querulously ask: might this not be just a holding action? In a department store last week I saw pot holders made of blue cloth. What, we must wonder, comes next? Aprons in a soccer design?

As a Third World country, we have merely been swept up in the running tide of this movement. The government has imported food and the private sector has imported heroin. The net result is people spending all their money on food or drugs, becoming bankrupt and ending up foraging in dustbins, thus exacerbating the state of bad public hygiene.

Now diarrhoea threatens the very fabric of our nation, especially jockey shorts.

In order to deal with this situation, I have drawn up a comprehensive two-point plan:

1. Import more toilet paper. The soft kind.

2. Build bigger and better public toilets. Easy availability of toilets is a basic human right.

Undoubtedly, there will be stringent opposition to this plan from some quarters. The trade unions will object on the grounds that we can make all the toilet paper we need right here. Obviously, though, this will not leave sufficient wood to construct the latrines. We must not forget that this is quintessentially an environmental issue and we need to conserve our forests. After all, we cannot build toilets in rural areas and real men, like bears of more temperate climes, excrete in the woods.

There will also be practical problems. Legislation will have to be passed ensuring people do not spend an inordinately long time in these toilets. As we know, there is no agony more acute than the man who is waiting to 'go'. There are certain cultural benefits, since Latin dancing was invented by Brazilians waiting to use the men's room at football games. Even in Trinidad, the dysentery outbreak has reduced crime since fewer people are able to leave their homes to be mugged and even when bandits come into a house where there are teenagers, they can never get into the bathroom.

I have never denied Brain's intellectual prowess. But, as I was to discover, intellect cannot compensate for a weak character. And Woman proved to be the downfall of this Adam. As usual.

To this day I do not understand Gwendolyn. Her attitude still mystifies – and even terrifies – me when I reflect on that entire situation. Did she, I still wonder, do what she did deliberately? Did she perhaps feel excluded from the relationship which was flourishing so greenly between Brain and myself? Or were her actions – for her – entirely natural?

I had had two more letters to the editor published and had even begun work on a pamphlet. Brain gave me much useful guidance and even criticized my sentence structure when necessary. He even – so quickly had our friendship ripened – told me about his Great

Accomplishment: a three-thousand-word short story he had submitted to an editor which, although rejected, had been accompanied by a personal note. 'When you understand this business,' said Brain, 'you will know how unusual it is to get a personal note with your rejection slip.'

'You never tried again?' I asked.

He shrugged. 'How many worlds can one man conquer?'

But I should tell the story in some order.

From my diary, I see that it was a Sunday that Brain invited me to go to the beach with Gwendolyn and himself. I wore a pair of blue and white tennis shorts, white jersey overlaid with purple abstracts and green shoes. We decided to go to Maracas.

Brain explained his reasons. 'Maracas beach,' he said, 'is in many ways a social hub of our society. There you will see many moods, many reflections, which you do not find in Mayaro, say, except on a long weekend. The young girls in bikinis represent a freedom in our society which we have not yet fully attained in the general political state despite the end of colonial rule.'

'I've never thought of it that way,' I said.

'Few persons had until I wrote a pamphlet on it,' he said. 'Did you bring the binoculars?'

'Yes.'

'Close observation is a skill which every aspiring writer needs to train in himself,' Brain explained. 'Even skilled but struggling artists like myself should always keep it honed.'

It was when we got into the car that I got my first shock. Gwendolyn was wearing shorts and a T-shirt and, as I leaned over to greet her, I saw her legs. It was the first time I had seen her in anything other than slacks or long skirts, and it was only my iron self-control that prevented me from gasping out loud. A lesser man would have reeled in shock.

How can I say this? To put it bluntly, Gwendolyn's legs were not shaved!

And, when I say they were not shaved, I do not mean she had

forgotten to shave that morning. I mean she had obviously never shaved her legs in her entire life!

From knees downward, her legs were a black mass of harsh, virgin curls. Even her thighs had some hair, though, thankfully, this was straight and relatively sparse. Here was a woman who clearly didn't need to have the slightest concern about any mosquito biting her legs, unless the mosquito had a sharp machete.

In the first, frozen seconds after this revelation, I struggled to find some rational explanation. Why, in a world full of razors, knives, even cutlasses, would a woman choose not to shave her legs? It could not be that her skin was sensitive – Gwendolyn was always scratching herself and her nails were quite long. It could not be religion – no merciful God, I knew, would ever have laid down a rule which forbade a woman to shave her legs.

Could it be, then, that she just found shaving too troublesome? I had heard women like this existed, but never thought I would actually meet one.

I must say I have always been proud of the manner in which I comported myself at that moment. My shocked silence could not have lasted more than a minute and then, tearing my gaze away from Gwendolyn's legs as though I had noticed nothing amiss, I said quite naturally, 'Hello, Gwendolyn. How are you?'

'Very well,' she answered. 'And yourself?'

'Shaven,' I said, the word just leaping to my lips.

'What?'

'Raving,' I said, quickly putting on an English accent.

Gwendolyn looked at me with some puzzlement, but only said, 'Brain's just gone to get the cooler.'

She ran her hands down her legs, with an awful rustling sound. I must say, though, that my first thoughts after the initial shock were not for myself, but for Brain. What terrible childhood trauma had he undergone, I wondered, which allowed him so easily to accept an unshaven woman as his wife? A Neanderthal might have been attracted to a hairy woman. So might Genghis Khan, Shaka Zulu and several species of ape. But these were all creatures who needed to keep warm at night. Surely Brain could have afforded a blanket. Gwendolyn was quite wealthy. Brain had told me that it was one of the reasons he married her. (Not that he was materialistic, but he needed to be free of financial worries in order to write full-time.) This explanation allowed me to ignore many of Gwendolyn's faults. But surely no amount of money, or devotion to one's art, could account for this!

I remembered then that Brain's father had died when he was still a boy. Perhaps, never having had the sensation of coarse hair, he now sought it in his wife. Perhaps, despite Brain's intellectual power and inimitable sophistication, there was a part of him that was still a little child.

That, I thought, as I watched him coming to the car carrying the cooler, must be it.

Only when we reached the beach did I discover the whole, horrible truth.

I do not clearly remember the details of that journey. Brain spoke with his usual eloquence on a number of issues even as he drove over the winding road to Maracas. (I had seen him walk and chew gum at the same time – in his own way, Brain was very much a Renaissance man.) But I was still trying to adjust to my new perspective on Gwendolyn and, by extension, Brain.

In a way, I suppose it was not her fault. Being Canadian, she might have been influenced by the French presence in that North American country. Europeans, having white skin, didn't even begin bathing regularly until the end of the 19th century. Indeed, although this is not mentioned in most history books, this was really why overpopulation was never a problem in the temperate nations. Thus, never having to buy clothes for growing children, they rapidly grew rich.

By contrast, in the land of my ancestors, people bathed regularly in the Ganges, had sex, and conceived so many children that they could never afford to save and invest. My theory was borne out by the fact that Brain and Gwendolyn had no children.

So we came to the beach, and I faced the second greatest challenge of my life. I have described my reaction when Selina showed up for my tea party in jeans. Now I faced a far greater trauma – to be seen in the company of a woman who, although just my friend's wife, was indubitably hairy-legged. With Selina, my great love had allowed me to face social disapprobation with something like equanimity. But now I had no such motive to bolster my flagging spirit. I searched my mind for some plausible excuse. And, as is so often the case, desperation brought inspiration.

'I'm going to get a Coke,' I said. 'I'll meet you all down the beach.'

'All right,' said Brain.

'Find an isolated spot, so I'll see you easily.'

'No problem.'

'Away from the crowd,' I said insistently.

'All right,' Brain said, looking at me a little sharply.

So they walked off and I went to one of the little sheds where drinks were sold. At least now I could pretend I had just met them by chance. And I would spend all day in the sea if I had to, just in case anyone I knew came along.

Eventually, when I thought a safe period of time had elapsed, I made my way down the beach. There were many people there, but Maracas is a fairly long beach and on the far side, to which Brain and Gwendolyn had repaired, were mostly sparse groups. I might get through this day yet. The thought of my many unconscious escapes over the past couple of months clutched at my heart like an icy hand. Suppose she had worn shorts to the mall? Brain, I thought, was clearly a man of unusual independence. Artists, I knew, often lived outside society's pale – but this was Bohemia on a grand scale.

In the distance I saw them. Brain was sitting on the bamboo beach mat in shorts and T-shirt. Gwendolyn had stripped to a dark blue one-piece bathing suit and was lying on her back, legs drawn up and arms linked behind her head. Brain gestured towards me and I waved back.

If there was one time I wished God had not blessed me with

perfect eyesight, as He has blessed me with so many other perfections, it was that time. I admit that at first I did not know what I was seeing. But the cause was mental rather than physical. I simply could not credit my senses. I thought that perhaps Gwendolyn was using some sort of black deodorant; I thought perhaps she had somehow spilled black paint down her arms; and finally, as I drew closer, I thought horrifiedly that two hairy spiders had crawled out of the sand and nestled in her armpits while she dozed unaware.

The truth, however, was far worse. *Gwendolyn did not shave her armpits.*

Everything went suddenly blank before my eyes. Dimly, I felt myself falling to the hot sand. I tried to put out my hands, but my mind seemed to have severed all connection with my body. The next thing I remember was Brain's anxious face above me.

'Paras, are you all right?' he asked.

Even in that extreme, my presence of mind was remarkable.

'A touch of the sun,' I said. 'I'm OK.'

With his help, I sat up, brushing sand off my clothes. I was careful not to look at Gwendolyn.

'Too much sun can deprive the body of essential minerals, salts and electrolytes,' Brain told me. 'That's probably why you fainted.'

'Yes,' I said.

But, in truth, I felt the first stirrings of anger within me. To be sure, there was no law which said a hairy woman might not go to the beach. But there was an ethical, as well as a legal, code. There was something, as I had learned in my fashion class at university, called Good Taste. And Gwendolyn had trespassed against this unwritten code. And Brain, maybe because as a writer he did not believe in anything which wasn't written down, had let her get away with it. Perhaps unfairly, I felt even angrier at Brain than Gwendolyn.

I spent much of that day apart from them both. (I did not go too far, since they were my ride home.) For hairy legs alone, I might have ignored social considerations. But hairy armpits went beyond mere neutrality. It was outright defiance, almost socio-pathic in nature. Several times that day, I saw small children pass by Gwendolyn and begin crying. Even some young women, seeing her, looked visibly upset.

And Brain just sat there indifferently!

The journey back home was mostly silent. I knew Brain was wondering why I had avoided them for most of the day. And what could I say? That I was afraid if I came too close to his wife I would become inextricably entangled? It was not a comment any man would have taken kindly to.

So I kept my peace and when we parted it was tacitly understood that we would not socialize again.

But that was not the end of the story.

For a long time after this, I was not sure if I should continue to pursue writing as a career. I had no doubt it would be immensely rewarding, for there were always companies which wanted to seem sophisticated. I could even marry a rich woman. But I was not certain I was willing to make the sacrifice such a goal required. To all outward appearances, Brain had a good relationship. His wife was both rich and white. Only those who were intimate with them would know the terrible truth. Sleeping with Gwendolyn must have been like wearing a hair-shirt.

Still, I did not immediately give up on writing, though I began paying more attention to sewing and fashion design. (Later, I would find a way to combine the two and both would have great influence on my illustrious career as Paras P.)

Ironically, my writing efforts actually began to progress more rapidly now I was no longer under Brain's stewardship. I had several more letters to the editor published and continued working sporadically on my pamphlet, which was entitled *Proper Dinner Etiquette and its Impact on the Moral Character* (later published as *Ethical Eating*).

Then I had a short story published in the *Trinidad Arts, Crafts and Knowledge Yearly* (*TACKY*) magazine.

To this day, I have no idea why Brain reacted to that story the way he did. But, given the furore the incident caused and the resultant publicity which has dogged me throughout my entire career, perhaps I should republish the story here to give readers a clear idea of the background to that infamous event.

The story is called 'Here, here' and deals with the inability of modern man to find his place in the world. It also deals with sexual roles. It is very existential. Oddly, the main character is a woman. This was what my creative instincts dictated, so it's not really my fault.

'Where am I?' said Amelia.

It was very dark.

'In a place beyond space or time,' replied the strange man with a big head.

'How did I end up in Haiti?' she asked.

'I have brought you here.'

'Where is here?'

'Everywhere and nowhere.'

'I lost my compass when my plane crashed.'

'You don't need a compass if you have faith in God.'

'You do if you want to find north on a dark night, sweetheart.'

'My love,' he said, 'leave this dangerous life. Why must a delicately nurtured woman like you fly over oceans?'

'Because I want to be as good as a man.'

'Kiss me,' he said.

'All right,' she said.

They kissed for a very long time.

'Something is tickling my mouth, dearest,' he said.

'That's my moustache, my love,' she answered. 'I told you I want to be a man. I think I've succeeded.'

The man screamed, trying to lose his erection.

The day after this story was published in *TACKY* Brain appeared in the classroom in which I was studying. It did not occur to me that he had been searching for me. Little did I know that he had read this story and become convinced it was an allusion to him. Why he should have felt so I have no idea.

He laid the magazine down in front of me.

'Paras, what is this?'

'It's a story . . .' I began, and then he hit me.

Brain, you must understand, was six inches taller than I and outweighed me by 150 pounds. Naturally, therefore, he made sure I was looking the other way and sitting down before he attacked me. He hit me three times before the other students were able to pull him off.

'He insulted my wife!' Brain screamed.

Luckily, all the blows were to the head and I was not seriously injured. But I had to go to the doctor and get three stitches for a cut below the eye. I have the scar to this day.

Brain left, muttering something about himself and Scott Fitzgerald. In my opinion, he was piqued because he realized I had moved beyond him.

The incident was carried in the paper the next day under the headline 'Battle of Words'. It brought me public attention in a way even my letters had not and undoubtedly helped launch the short professional career as a journalist which laid the foundation for my later, truer role in the world.

Chapter Five

I am the trumpet-voice, the Stentor.
I am the whisperer, the Mentor.

From 'Advertising' by
A.S.J. Tessimond

After this fiasco, as I like to call it, I threw myself into my work with renewed vigour. This enabled me, along with about 3,000 other people, to obtain my university degree. I was fortunate, however, in that only about 600 of those persons had a degree like mine. It was called a General degree, and showed we were well-rounded individuals, fit for any task or, as most employers seemed to think, none.

As I entered the job market, this fact struck me again and again. As a body, employers did not seem to appreciate that, while it was true I had no special skills, I could quote Shakespeare. But the government, as always, was indifferent to cultural attainment. This is one reason I have always favoured the colonial system, where at least gentlemen were appreciated.

Most of my compatriots were swallowed up by the teaching service. Indeed, to this day some have never been found. I heard stories, though, which said that if you passed by some schools in the middle of the day, you would see a lonely, haggard figure at the front of a classroom and hear the eerie squeak of chalk. I do not say I gave credence to such tales; I merely repeat what I heard.

I, of course, had no intention of becoming a teacher. It was not that I held the profession in contempt. Jesus, after all, was a teacher. But He had only to deal with Roman soldiers, bloodthirsty mobs and being nailed to a cross. A classroom of teenagers was an entirely different proposition. It was not, mind you, that I was a coward. Had Jesus's position been offered to me, I would have accepted it cheerfully. After all, being the Son of God does carry with it a certain status and the hours weren't too bad. (Jesus, you will notice, hardly worked nights and, when he did, it was mostly suppers.) Being nailed to a cross could not have been pleasant, but at least there is Valium nowadays.

However, I certainly wasn't going to face a classroom of forty or so noisy teenagers for a paltry $36,000 a year. In fact, there was one ad which I answered just in case there was something in it. Some might say I was foolish to do so but, given my later career as Paras P. and my notable spiritual success in it, you never know. It is, after all, a miraculous world. I am still waiting for a reply and who knows? Perhaps those who placed the ad might notice my application here – hence my reason for writing it again – even though it was overlooked in the rush which undoubtedly occurred so many years ago. They are probably processing the letters still. Naturally, I told God nothing about this, though I still continued having personal revelations.

I first saw this ad in the 'Situations Vacant' columns in the classified section of the daily newspapers. It read:

Applications are hereby invited for the position of Supreme Being. An exciting project involving the creation of a new reality is about to be launched. This has become necessary since the old reality does not appear to be functioning too well.

The successful applicant must be willing to work overtime, though not longer than eternity, and must have a sense of order. Logic is essential, since we are seeking to create a reality as far removed from this one as possible.

Little or no sense of humour is also desirable since, as

evidenced by giraffes, marriage and Third World debt, this reality has already suffered from the incumbent's wit. The only people who think this reality makes sense are those who think murder helps put hair on the chest.

We have a competent staff which will oversee the actual physical construction of the new universe. While most details will remain the same, height will be increased a little, since short men are entirely useless in this reality. Women have also been given a raw deal and, in the new universe, cellulite will simply not exist. The main function of the Supreme Being will be to give a sense of purpose and meaning to the conscious inhabitants of the new reality. This will be the major difference between this reality and the old.

The successful applicant will have to be extremely disciplined and refrain from destroying the planet when people don't listen. A Supreme Being cannot have everything Her way. For example, Her – or His – image will be multiplied by the thousands and most of the interpretations of Her or His words will be wrong.

Creating prophets through virgin births – besides being absolutely no fun – will not help change this. Nail-paring is a necessary prerequisite for God. We do not want to see children lying torn on rubble for a noun. The job carries great responsibility and there is no pension plan. The successful applicant may find it better to pretend She or He does not exist.

While this is obviously no easy role, the position does have several benefits, including omnipotence and complimentary tickets to all Rolling Stones concerts. If interested, write The Pantheon, Many Mansions, and then burn your application. Suitable applicants will be contacted in due course and should walk with a toothbrush.

Although there were many things in this ad which I did not understand, I still thought it worthwhile to apply. Somebody even told

me it was a joke published by an atheist after Islamic fundamen-
talists started pointing out that killing men, women and children
was a moral duty. But I did not believe this, for would anyone risk
the wrath of God for people stupid enough to live in a desert? I
didn't think so, and discounted this story. In any case, as I always
say, you never know; and I certainly didn't want to risk missing a
God-given chance through my ignorance. Perhaps I was wasting my
time but, to coin a phrase, nothing ventured, nothing gained. If, by
some chance, God did want to retire, I was at least as well-
qualified as some to fill the post, as you will see from my application.

> Dear Pantheon [I wrote]
>   I hereby apply for the position of Supreme Being, unless
> that is some new ice-cream flavour. I do not think I am better
> than anyone else, but I have no allergies and I am a virgin. I
> have lived a good, almost godly, life and I am highly
> intelligent. My lack of humour is also a byword among my
> acquaintances. I like Mick Jagger and believe I will handle
> omnipotence with little or no difficulty.
>   Thanking you in advance,
>   Paras Parmanandansingh.

This application, I felt, was bound to be at least as good as anyone
else's on the planet, although I must admit to hoping that Nelson
Mandela or Raquel Welch had not seen the ad. I followed
instructions precisely in submitting it and, although I have received
no answer yet, who knows what might happen once I cross to the
Other Side?

At any rate, although that job didn't immediately pan out, my
first position was relatively close. I became an Information Officer
for the government.

The story of how I won this important post is an interesting
one. I had, of course, been looking for jobs for many weeks. It
was no easy task, given the economic decline the country was then
experiencing. Not a day passed when I did not wake up early in

the morning, go out and buy papers, and open them immediately at the classified sections. Sometimes my entire morning would be spent on the telephone and even, in the evening when the sun wasn't so hot, writing out application letters. My father, loving though he was, got quite tired of seeing me around the house. But he knew I was trying.

I went to several interviews without success. I could not figure out what was wrong. I spoke properly, my pimples had mostly cleared up and my hair had been waved. Needless to say, I was always impeccably dressed. I wore blue, grey, black, green three-piece suits and ties which reflected the entire spectrum. All to no avail.

So what was the problem? There was, I realized, something missing. There had to be a secret to success, but what was it? I even ordered a pamphlet through the mail, called *The Secret to Success*. It had, I admit, some useful advice. 'Be born a white American,' advised the author. 'Being born Japanese is even better, but then you will have short legs.'

He went on to deal with such usual business precautions as keeping two sets of books, giving a false name, and working through the mail. But this advice, though good, did not affect my immediate situation.

And then, as I was perusing a magazine one day, I saw the answer staring me right in the face. I had the hair, I had the suits, I had the teeth. *But I did not have a briefcase!*

So true it is that we never perceive that which is most obvious. And, having realized what was missing, things fell in place almost miraculously. My father came the very next day and told me he had fixed up an interview with a friend of his who had a cousin who had a brother in the Information Ministry.

'I need a briefcase,' I told him.

'You don't need a briefcase,' he said, in his typically old-fashioned manner.

'Yes, I do,' I said, 'or else I won't get this job.'

He threw up his hands.

'Oh, all right. Anything to get you out the blasted house.'

He was joking, of course. He knew I'd never rent a place when I could stay at home, and get free meals and my clothes washed.

So he bought me my first briefcase. It was second-hand, but it was extremely elegant. Genuine black plastic covering. Combination lock. Contoured handle. It even had a chain and handcuff, which gave me a strange thrill.

My interview was successful. I wore my black suit with a red shirt and white socks, which were the colours of the national flag. Add the briefcase, and the result was a foregone conclusion. The interviewer naturally figured that a man with a briefcase like mine would be an asset to any organization. They could feel safe entrusting their business to me. (The handcuff and chain, I thought, probably clinched it.) As I walked along the streets that day, I could see from the respectful glances people gave me that they thought I had important papers in my briefcase. In fact, it contained my lunch, my birth certificate and a pack of cards. And, to tell you what a difference the briefcase made, when I sat down at the Savannah to eat my lunch, I was even approached by a woman.

The perceptive reader is undoubtedly saying to herself that it might not have been the briefcase, but my clothes and other natural attributes which caused this woman to approach me. I have no doubt that my attractive appearance was a factor, but consider her first words to me.

'That's a nice briefcase,' she said.

She wore a red miniskirt, red lipstick and reddened hair. A colour-coordinated woman.

I smiled modestly. 'Thank you,' I answered.

'What you have in it?' she asked.

'Oh, just some papers.'

'Important ones?'

'Yes.' After all, my birth certificate was important.

'I could tell,' she said softly.

'Oh? How?' I asked.

'I saw the handcuff.'

'Oh,' I said.

She moved a little closer to me on the bench. Her eyes were looking straight into mine, and for one uncomfortable moment I wondered if there was *yampee* in their corners.

'I just love handcuffs,' she said.

'What?' I said. I hadn't heard her because she had spoken a little breathily.

'I said, I just *love* handcuffs,' she repeated.

'Oh,' I said, a little puzzled. Maybe, I thought, she had great respect for law and order. And then another, more stimulating thought occurred to me – maybe she liked men in uniform! I suddenly wished fervently I were a policeman. Even a postal uniform would have done. Her next words seemed to confirm my impression.

'Where do you work?'

'What?' I said again, wishing she wouldn't put so much air in her voice when she spoke.

'Where you working?' she said.

'I work at the Information Ministry,' I said, which was practically true since I was starting the following Monday. I have never believed in being ruled by schedules, in any case.

She stroked a forefinger slowly along my forearm. Was this, I wondered nervously, foreplay?

'So is there lots of private information you'd like to tell me?' she said. 'Maybe if we went somewhere more . . . private?'

And only then did I realize what was really going on! I cursed myself for a fool not to have picked up on it earlier.

'I have to go now,' I said suddenly, and walked off without a backward glance.

Perhaps I could have handled the situation better. But, remember, I was young and inexperienced. Were it not for that, I would have realized at once what the woman was. I do not know if she was working for the private media or, as was more likely, the opposition. She may even have been an independent agent, selling what information she could get to the highest bidder. But I told her nothing. And, as I walked home, I realized how much responsibility rested on my shoulders. Information was power, and I was an information officer. In my hands, as much as in the hands of the prime minister, rested the fate of my nation.

I should have had that woman arrested. But of course she could always have argued that it was my sophisticated appearance which had attracted her – a story which would have been difficult to disprove. That night, for my own protection, I wrote a detailed report of what had occurred.

The next few nights were restless ones for me. Would I, I wondered, be able to handle the portfolio I had been given? I had been able to resist the red-dressed woman successfully, but I have never been very partial to the colour red. Suppose an attractive woman dressed in yellow – my favourite colour – approached me for high-level information. If I knew what she was up to, I was sure my moral strength would help me resist her blandishments. But how could I know? Suddenly, I had been catapulted into a shadowy world where motives were unclear, words were noise hiding meaning and one looked for the masks on every human face. I felt like a character in a Le Carré novel, trapped in an obscure world of convoluted prose.

Then, on the Sunday before I had to go to work, I had an inspiration. Given the day, I am sure it was divinely inspired. I woke up and had breakfast. But, on a strange impulse, instead of my usual orange juice and vodka, I made myself a martini. Shaken, not stirred. And suddenly I felt like a new man. A man named Bond. James Bond.

And why not? Why should my world be dark and lonely? I was an information officer, dammit. I would be attending high-level meetings, international conferences and cocktail parties with public figures. I would get to know all sorts of people and, as the saying goes, it wasn't what you knew, but who you knew. There were all sorts of opportunities beckoning to me, and an exciting life.

I wondered if I'd get a badge.

I will skip lightly over the early aspects of my training. I spent the first few weeks reading the basic training manuals: *The Prince*, *How to Lie with Statistics*, *Complete Superlatives* and *Goebbels – The Master at Work*.

Only after this training period was over was I allowed actually to begin helping disseminate information to the general public. At first this consisted in merely checking public signs and notices to make sure they were spelt correctly and clearly worded. It had me on the road a lot and I drank plenty of beer. However, it also made my right arm become tanned from resting on the car door. To a lesser extent, the right side of my face also tanned and, when speaking to important people, I had to remember to present my better, or left, side.

I progressed rapidly and, within a year, was writing notices about bridges or roads being closed for repairs, electricity being turned off for repairs, water being turned off for repairs. There was generally quite a lot to do. However, I approached my task with enthusiasm and a large spelling dictionary. My competence must have been noted because, in less than two years, I was moved to writing announcements of government seminars, meetings and conferences. This was less taxing, but required greater care. Oscar Wilde once wrote that the poet can survive anything but a misprint. Similarly, the writer of releases can survive anything but a wrong date. I strove my best to make my releases as informative, accurate and interesting as possible – a more difficult task than the layman might imagine. In fact, it was a tribute to my skill that these releases often appeared unchanged in the newspapers. Thus, the clippings I have preserved for posterity in my files are entirely my own work and, save in a very few cases, the purity of my prose has been in no way corrupted by the editor's pencil.

I moved up the ranks quite rapidly. There was in me a burning ambition, a desire to do my job as well as possible, which brought me to the attention of my superiors. In fact, I once overheard the information comptroller, Dr Charles Drayton, conversing with the supervisor of ministerial releases about me. As had become my useful habit, I taped the conversation.

'My boots have been really shiny since Paras started working here,' he said, laughing. He was Guyanese so I didn't quite understand his metaphor, although he was clearly happy about my efficiency.

The supervisor agreed. 'I make sure and sit down whenever he's around,' he said, nodding. I felt quite elated knowing that the supervisor had so much confidence in me that he felt no need even to get up once I was present.

It was not too long before I was attending official functions and writing them up for the newspapers, television and radio. My literary talent stood me in good stead in this area. Writing about social functions is both a trained skill and an art. It is not a job for the novice. Not only must you be able to get the names of all the important people present, but you must know who the important people are. Then, when writing about the occasion, you must know what to mention and what to leave out. This is the essence of art. So many beginner writers make the mistake of trying to put in everything. No, no, no. You must pick, choose, construct. Yet you must also be able to convey the atmosphere – the enjoyment or interest or importance of the function. Moreover, you must be able to do this even if the function, as so often happens, wasn't enjoyable, interesting or important. As one of my training manuals put it: 'The only difference between writing Official Information in a positive manner and writing fiction is that fiction requires greater accuracy.'

I think my greatest advantage as an information officer was that I believed what I wrote, or thought it should be believed. After all, one could not have government ministers being embarrassed by their own mistakes. Embarrassment can easily become political destabilization, especially given the number of gaffes politicians tend to make. It was my duty as an Information Officer to prevent this.

I remember one particular case, when Minister N., not his real initial, who at the time held the tourism portfolio, singlehandedly paralysed the island's tourism industry for several years. Of course, thanks to the diligent efforts of the Information Ministry and myself, the public never knew this.

We were at a special function in Miami. The Americas Development Bank had just loaned our government US$172 million in order to develop the tourism sector. In gratitude, our government decided to have a formal reception costing about one million dollars to thank the bank. Quite normal protocol. But, with champagne flowing so freely and being in a different country and with no media present, the minister naturally let his hair down. In fact, I don't think he ever found his hairpins afterwards, but I was able to charge this to official expenditure.

He also got so drunk that he went about pinching the bottoms of all the women present and, while some of them should have been grateful to have any man pinching their bottoms, many were not too pleased. But the real trouble occurred when the minister got up to make the feature address. He was so drunk, he found he couldn't see straight and so he decided to ignore his speech and talk off the top of his head. And, of course, when a politician tries talking off the top of his head, he invariably ends up talking through his hat. I still have the recording.

'We are very grateful to the ADB for giving us one hundred million dollars to develop tourism,' Minister N. begins.

'One hundred and seventy-two,' somebody calls out.

'Somebody told me it was 172, which is true – excuse my poetry – but naturally palms have had to be greased along the way.' He spits. 'This palm,' he said. 'And then I had to pay off my left palm so it wouldn't know what my right palm was doing,' he adds with a giggle. 'This kind of thing runs into money.'

There is a brief pause as one of the minister's aides whispers to him.

'But I was talking about tourism. Why, you ask, am I talking about tourism? 'Cause I'm the damned tourism minister and that's how I earn my salary. By trying to get you people to come to my country. We have sun all year round – but I hear you does worry about skin cancer. We have beautiful beaches, but I hear all-you worrying about the environment. Like white people don't have nothing else to do but worry.'

Again there is a brief pause while the minister's aides confer with him. There is a slight scuffle.

'So what it have left? Well, wining. But all-you don't know what wining is.'

'Speak in English,' says an American voice.

'When you start, I will start,' the minister answers. He appears pleased by this retort, because he laughs heartily and repeats it 12 times.

Nonetheless, he does make some attempt to speak in his usual polished manner from this point. But this is difficult since, from the clattering sounds, he apparently keeps falling off the podium.

' "Wining",' he says, 'is the national dance of Trinidad. But you need not drink wine or even use a crank in order to do it. It involves a circular or rotary motion of the hips. Visitors who wish to see wining before the actual two-day carnival can go to any of the many public fêtes or steel band competitions. Wining of a slightly different order can also be seen in "chutney" dancing, as practised among the island's East Indian community. However, this should not be attempted by amateurs since serious injury can result.'

The minister pauses, apparently having forgotten what he was going to say. Then he remembers the island's tourist slogan. 'Be nice, it's nice,' he says, and you can tell he is beaming at his own cleverness.

'But,' he continues, 'it is no use telling you about wining. We need to teach it to you. In fact,' his voice rises, 'wining is our gift to the industrialized world. So many of your countries have negative population growth. You think it's because you have birth control and because middle class people don't want more children than cars in the family. No, no, no,' he says, repeating it about 33 times. 'No, no, no,' he ends, just as the audience is beginning to grow restive. 'The real reason is because you white people cannot wine. That means there is a qualitative difference between the sex you have and the sex we have. Maybe it's body shape – earlier tonight I was pinching some bottoms, and I missed several times. That would never have happened in Trinidad because Trini women have lovely bumsees.

'If you white people can learn to wine, you will enjoy sex a lot more, make more white children and, if you have any sense of parental responsibility at all, send them to Trinidad to learn to wine, too.

'In fact, if I had my way, I'd set up a wining institute with this money. We need modern research – computer-generated motion studies, analyses of synovial fluid, surgical methods to discover why white people's rib-cages are fused to their pelvic girdles. And I'd be happy to run the institute. Hell, yes!'

And, to sporadic and uncertain applause, Minister N., judging from the thud, collapses gracefully on to the stage.

Needless to say, we never got the loan.

When we came back to Trinidad, I was part of the team which had to draw up an official report of the trip for public consumption. After much brainstorming, consultation and consumption of rum, we came up with the following.

The recent failure of the Government to access a $172 million loan from the Americas Development Bank can be traced directly to the positions adopted by local trade union leaders, the decline in world tourism and our colonial history.

Although Minister N. made a brilliant presentation, his sterling performance was undone by all these factors. Some

94

ADB officials, we regret to say, were close-minded and even inebriated. Yet the minister, in describing all our country's natural attractions, and even giving a practical demonstration to the gathering – one ADB official was heard to remark 'Fascinating!' – won the admiration and approbation of all the ADB officials and their wives. Nonetheless, the Government team was told in no uncertain terms that, because of the ideological position adopted by trade unions, this country could not be considered a secure debtor for tourist loans.

The Government was told that one of our union leaders, whom we shall not name since we do not wish to cast stones, had described the tourist industry as a form of re-colonialism. 'This,' said one ADB official, 'is very worrisome.'

On his return, Minister N. said, 'I am, of course, extremely disappointed. But I cannot tell trade union leaders what to say. After all, this is a democracy. I would implore them, however, to be more careful about their statements and consider how their pronouncements can affect our international status. In any case, our problems here are no different from problems anywhere else in the world and, if the world isn't making it, why should we?'

It was after this effort, into which I had a major input, that I was promoted to the Damage Control Department (known in-house as Bullshitters Inc.). I was to prove remarkably talented at my job. It was for me a signal triumph. My career seemed to have taken off, and I dreamed of reaching untold heights. Perhaps even main speech writer for the prime minister. And, from writing the prime minister's speeches to being prime minister, how long a step could it be? In politics, after all, the important thing is not what you do, but what you say you are going to do. The only question in my mind then was whether I wanted to be the power behind the throne or on the throne itself. Both had advantages, but sitting on the throne got you on television regularly. And for some time I pondered one of the central philosophical questions of our century: does a man truly exist if he has not been photographed? Or been on the news at eleven? Or at least been heard on the radio? In this regard, women are lucky: they just have a baby or two and their reality is confirmed. For what can be more real, more intense, than bringing a new life into this world, unless it's getting high, low, hang jack and game in all-fours?

As circumstances turned out, though, I was never to become speech writer for the prime minister or even prime minister. The issue was decided for me by a Higher Power, and perhaps was for the best.

The apex of my career as an Information Officer undoubtedly came with the Great Sucouyant Controversy, as it has come to be known. So, like Icarus, did I fly highest before falling. So has it been since the beginning of history. As God told me once, Adam was having the best sex in his life before being cast out of the Garden of Eden and forced to start a family.

Older readers may remember the events which outraged the entire nation for ten days, which was one day more than the official record. It was the weekly newspapers – thank God they are not published daily – which first began investigating reports of a shortage of blood in individuals around the country. (*Sucouyant*, I should mention for the benefit of my many foreign admirers, is the local term for a vampire.) The government was, naturally, very dismayed when documents were uncovered which suggested that party officials had been selling blood illegally to paper American companies. The minister of trade told me so himself.

'We very dismayed,' he said. 'I don't know how the newspapers could have got those documents.'

'What about the blood selling?' I asked.

He shrugged. 'I guess it will have to stop,' he said. He looked at me closely. 'Can we trust you, Paras?'

'Minister!' I said, shocked. The minister knew that I had never ruffled any feathers, made any waves or even rocked the boat. I could have become a cliché without even a written test.

'I'm sorry,' he apologized. 'But could you handle this?'

'Leave it to me, minister,' I said confidently. Little did I know then how this would return to haunt me in later years.

The task I faced was no easy one. The government had already made the mistake of following standard procedures. They had denied the accusations and accused the media of exaggerating the situation. The minister himself said they were misinterpreting the information and threatened legal action. (For aspirants to public office, these standard steps are laid out in the *Civil Service Regulations*, 1894.)

But the issue gained too much publicity for these measures to be effective. It was then that I was called in.

It took an entire week, working day and night, before my report was ready. Because of the highly confidential nature of my task, I also had to work alone.

My final report is too lengthy to reproduce here. However, the student of history, or a student of politics, may find the background of interest.

The first thing I did was to gather some relevant reference books. Besides the obvious *Blood Types and Analysis*, I also used *How to Write Reports* and a companion volume, *Factual Reporting – A Political Oxymoron*. I also brought out my personal copy of *Sewing Covers for Fun and Profit*. Two volumes I found extremely useful were by an ex-government minister: *The Laws of Trinidad and How to Ignore Them* and *Party Chairmanship: The Road to Riches*. Another essential text for official reports on controversial issues is, of course, the oft-used *Shelf and Cupboard Building*.

On my recommendation, the prime minister appointed a one-man 'Commission (Civil Service Response 27D) to Investigate the Incidence of Blood Loss in Citizens'. He was of course just a figurehead, and I did the real work.

The conclusion of the commissioner's report shows how effectively I was able to defuse the situation. Much of it is my own wording:

> Following the guidelines did not prove to be the most onerous part of my task. Once the persons being interviewed understood that their own skins were at stake, it was easy to free the Minister and Government of all blame.
>
> Luckily, too, no blood sales had been recorded and I was able to raise irrelevant queries about the manner of collecting it. I was also able to point out that Government Ministers, because of the stress of their jobs, need more blood than ordinary citizens. I also raised ethical questions about the public, especially young children, being exposed to the pernicious influence of television shows, like *Night Stalker* and *Dallas*, and to Government documents. Clearly, this needless fuss proves the public's inability to handle information and justifies the covers I have sewn for these documents.
>
> However, it was ensuring future security which provided real problems, since, as a person of limited manual skill, building a shelf for this report presented some challenges. I also found difficulty building a skeleton-sized cupboard, but was able to do so after getting the shirt sizes of several Government Ministers.
>
> I am confident that the standard dust provided by your goodly self will remain undisturbed for many years.
>
> A.B.O. Treyfuss (Major, Rtd.)

This, as I say, was the signal triumph of my life up to that point. It seemed to me that no doors were closed to me from this time on. But I was soon to learn how cruel, how callous, the world of politics can be.

After the Great Sucouyant Controversy, I was given several important assignments. These included explaining why the finance minister had been forgiven a ten million dollar loan by a bank the government held shares in, why the education minister had written a letter of recommendation for a child abuser and why a drug baron was driving around in a car formerly owned by the prime minister.

But these were all relatively easy tasks. (Vested interests were seeking to undermine the finance minister because of the excellent job he was doing and, hey, we all have fiscal problems; the education minister knew the abuser's father, a well-respected businessman and, hey, children can't be coddled in today's world; surely you don't believe your *prime minister* is involved with drug traffickers?)

But then came the Great Hibiscus Controversy.

You should understand that the ruling political party used hibiscus flowers as their party symbol. They decorated their headquarters with it, made clothes with hibiscus patterns, and even made tie-pins in the shape of a hibiscus.

It was these tie-pins, and the president of the United States of America, which fuelled the furore.

The government parliamentarians wore their tie-pins everywhere, but especially at official functions. The idea was to make no distinction between party and government so citizens wouldn't get any progressive ideas about democracy and political principle.

Naturally, therefore, our prime minister made certain to have a new tie-pin made when he was invited to meet the US president. Everything went well. The prime minister made a brilliant speech, which had been written for him by Khomeini '1984' Hosein. In his speech, entitled 'Economic turnaround in developing nations, or the serpent bites the heel that stamps him', the prime minister pointed out the dire need for rich countries to give more aid to poorer ones if they didn't want our citizens to turn to drug-trafficking and make more addicts in the richer countries.

It was a persuasive, well thought-out argument and he received lusty applause, primarily from a blonde prostitute hired for the occasion. But when he leaned over to have a few words with the

99

US president, the prime minister's tie-pin, most unfortunately, inflicted a nasty flesh wound on the president's cheek.

It was the moment the opposition had been waiting for. Why, they asked, should government ministers wear the party symbol everywhere?

'It sets off my clothes, adding to my appearance,' said the culture minister, who was one of the first persons to respond.

This answer only worsened matters. The culture minister was a strikingly unattractive woman, whose looks could have been improved only by a designer paper bag. To argue, therefore, that a hibiscus tie-pin improved her appearance seemed the height of political hypocrisy.

'Can a hibiscus tie-pin truly go with anything?' asked the opposition chief whip, Savita Sackal, placing the matter on an even wider plane.

And so the accusations and counter-accusations began. Motions were moved in parliament, the letters pages were filled with nothing else, endless news conferences were held and several gardens were vandalized.

Before the issue got entirely out of hand, the information minister called me in.

'Settle this, Paras,' he told me, before taking his afternoon nap.

But it was easier said than done, which, now that I think about it, was probably why he asked me to do it. The issue, it seemed to me, was raging like a bushfire. What, then, could I do to control this conflagration? The reader will understand how naïve I still was when I decided that an expert appraisal might defuse the matter.

I still hold that my analysis, as far as it went, was not wrong. It seemed to me that the issue of tie-pins was only apparently one about democratic values. The core of the controversy, however, centred around something far more important to the human heart – to wit, style.

Settle the issue of whether the hibiscus tie-pin was fashionable or not, I thought, and the controversy would die a natural death.

I realized, however, that in order for this approach to be effective, there would have to be a semblance of objectivity. The issue had already been aired so widely that normal PR techniques, such as mere insistence, hyperbole or outright deception, would not work. I had to adopt a journalistic approach. And this was to prove my undoing (although it also became my eventual salvation – truly, there is a power which looks after good men).

I did several interviews with leading fashion experts on the island. I had, of course, established important contacts when I did my sewing course at university. The information minister passed it after a quick glance during his all-fours game, then hanged a jack. The article I wrote appeared in all the leading newspapers, and was broadcast on television and radio. Not even my 'Sucouyant report' had received so much airplay. It was the greatest moment of my life, and I am not ashamed to say that I bought 200 copies of each paper, and made several video and audio recordings.

The article was put out as an official release from the Information Ministry, and read as follows.

After the latest controversy to erupt in parliament, we thought we should hear what experts in the local fashion industry have to say on the matter.

Leading clothes designer Choo Choo Chu described himself, in all modesty, as a penetrating person. Several of his closest colleagues in the theatre agree wholeheartedly.

His qualifications reinforce this opinion, as do his leather pants. Mr Chu, or, as he prefers to be called, Choo Choo, holds several international diplomas in fashion design, cosmetology and hairstyling. He has put on shows in New York, London and Paris and once made eye contact with Elsa Klensch at a party in Tokyo. Choo Choo backs up his expertise with ten years' experience, enormous creativity and a lovely complexion.

When we visited his home for this interview – Choo Choo dislikes talking on the telephone because, he says, 'The *personal touch* is so important, don't you think?' – he was dressed in his trade mark pink leather jeans, a black silk top and purple sandals. It was obvious that his insights into the present political controversy would prove invaluable.

Nor were we disappointed. In that direct way of his, Choo Choo immediately got down to what he calls the nitty gritty or, if he's feeling slightly S&M, brass tacks.

'The fundamental question,' he said, 'is whether a hibiscus tie-pin is aesthetically pleasing or not. This, in turn, leads to the important question of aesthetics itself.'

He drew himself as an example, using oil pastels. 'I am, of course, one of the most truly beautiful men – I hope my feminist friends will excuse me using that hated noun, but I do wear leather jackets – in the Caribbean. But beauty, even beauty such as mine, is created and not merely given.'

This was indeed a shocking revelation. But Choo Choo merely sipped calmly at his mint julep and explained: 'There are those who argue that just because the hibiscus is a floral design, it *must* be aesthetically pleasing. I question this assumption. Contrary to popular belief, nature does not always have a sense of beauty. Look, for example, at Sai Baba. Should he really be wearing an orange robe with that face?

'The truth is, Nature sometimes plays these little jokes. The hibiscus is an example of such humour. It is not balanced. There is an intrinsic lack of cosmic harmony in its design. This is what one must look for, yet it is rarely found either in nature or men's restrooms.'

But the second fashion expert we contacted disagreed. Patricia LaFemme, owner of a leading boutique and casual dog-breeder, said, 'I wouldn't want to get into personalities, but Choo Choo Chu hasn't really designed anything noteworthy for the past ten years. Moreover, his interior decorator, Kawal, whom he hired just because they have a personal relationship, did a perfectly awful job on his living room. Chu's opinion on the hibiscus is, therefore, quite suspect.'

Pat has been designing clothes since she was four years old and says she has been in the business 15 years now. Behind the mascara, she undoubtedly looks young for her age. She became a leader in the industry virtually by accident, she says, when she got pregnant for a married businessman. With the money he gave her, she opened her boutique, *Pat Non Male*, which caters exclusively for women who like spending rich men's money. The store was quite crowded when we arrived for the interview.

'I think it is rather bold-faced of Chu to place himself above nature in aesthetic matters. In my opinion, the hibiscus tie-pin can only enhance the appearance of parliamentarians, although a hibiscus hood would probably do an even better job.'

Pat admitted that opposition Chief Whip Savita Sackal has some fashion sense, a nice smile and would look thrilling in black leather. 'But that doesn't change the fact that she's quite short,' she pointed out. She thinks Savita's criticism was a political mistake. 'Miss Sackal seems to me to be a confident, intellectual woman with a social conscience. She is clearly not qualified to make it in the fashion world.'

Attempts to contact the American First Lady proved futile. The views of the US president were not sought since he does not choose his own ties. This, significantly, is done through acts of Congress.

The objective reader will agree that this was a well-researched, thoroughly balanced article. In fact, at the time I considered it the best thing I had ever written. It seemed to me that my art had attained a new level, gaining a depth and substance it had never before possessed, rather like good loam.

Picture my shock, therefore, when early the next morning I was hauled up on the carpet before the information minister, getting some pretty nasty burns in the process.

I will not describe the scene which followed in any detail. The information minister used some opprobrious terms which, though recorded, I do not wish to recall. Suffice to say that the powers-that-were were extremely displeased with my effort. They felt I had undermined their position by making an objective presentation of the issue.

'When we want facts, we'll invent them!' the minister roared at me. 'When we want expert opinions, we'll buy them!'

And so I was dismissed forthwith. They were able to do that because, thanks to civil service bureaucracy, I had never been confirmed in my post. I had by then worked in the Information Ministry for seven years. If I had lasted two more, my appointment would have been confirmed and they would never have got me out. (When civil servants do fail in their duty, they are just suspended with full pay and become taxi-drivers.) But, as it turned out, leaving the Information Ministry was the best thing that could have happened to me. If I had not, I might never have become, albeit for a short time, a full-fledged journalist.

Chapter Six

Perhaps my semblance might deceive the truth
That I to manhood am arrived so near,
And inward ripeness doth much less appear,
Than some more timely-happy spirits endu'th.

From Sonnet VII by John Milton

I was now thirty years old and unemployed. My father had lost the last council election and so could do nothing for me. Not, of course, that I would have let him. But he had made enough money so that, if I wanted, I could have stayed at home quite comfortably and become a great writer. I spent much of my time reading in those days, and writing immortal prose did not seem to me too difficult an ambition. All you needed was a thesaurus, an eye for minute detail and a high forehead. And my hairline had already begun receding a little. But I knew I was destined for better things.

This spurred me on to look for work. I was also worried in case the sight of me sitting around the house all day doing nothing drove my father to an early grave. He was a man who believed in the old-fashioned values of hard work, frugality and beer-drinking. I had inherited this need to work from him, once I could do it in an air-conditioned office and didn't have to leave my desk too often.

Several events conspired to help me find a new job in a very short space of time. First, a weekly paper found out about my being fired because of my hibiscus article and they carried a short piece on it called 'Abuse of flower power'. I do not know how they came by the details – possibly, I had mentioned it casually to a reporter from the paper when I called him up.

Second, the same week the story was carried, the person who had been indirectly responsible for my losing my job – Choo Choo Chu – launched his summer collection which featured the revolutionary 'floating collar'.

And third, the fashion editor at the same paper died. This, I later found out, was something the paper had been waiting on for a long time. The lady in question was in late middle age and had skin which would have made any self-respecting prune turn green with envy. Yet she insisted on having her picture published with all her articles, thus causing readers to spend fruitless hours trying to smooth the page out. It reduced newspaper sales considerably, I was told, but the woman owned shares in the paper so they couldn't fire her. She wrote a fashion column every week praising the styles of the 50s and wondering what fashion had come to. She might have lived on to become an old hag, but luckily she drowned one night while sleeping in her bathtub. She had been doing this for years, it turned out, because sleeping in a bed gave her bedsores. So the secret of her marvellously wrinkled skin was finally known, and was mentioned in her obituary.

My reporter friend told me about the position and I immediately offered to cover Choo Choo's opening for them.

'Better you than me,' said the editor, Kenneth Wolf, with a grin. He apparently didn't care for fashion reporting.

The launch was quite a gala affair. It was held at Stollmeyer's Castle, which is really a tall old house with lots of wooden turrets, and the place was festooned with brightly coloured balloons and masses of crêpe paper. The pundits of the fashion world were all present, wearing dhotis. A statue of Gandhi – to whom I was later sometimes compared, though, obviously, my knees were not as bony – had just been erected in Adam Smith square, so dhotis were big in Trinidad. I myself wore dragon-red pyjama-style trousers with matching jacket and open-toed sandals. (I was never one to follow the crowd, unless they were looking at a fatal accident.)

The fashion experts were all abuzz with excitement, for rumour had it that Choo Choo had something extra special planned. And, when the first model, Darryl, came out, there was a great 'ahh' of excitement, astonishment and, from some of the more sensitive members of the select audience, orgasm.

Darryl wore a lovely shirt in shimmering green artificial silk and, drifting above him, was Choo Choo's unique innovation – the floating collar. One immediately thought of green seas and the melancholy seaweed that floats among the cold waves. Yet, as Darryl made his way down the catwalk, the collar floating behind him, a new feeling superseded. Wasn't Choo Choo trying to say that, just as the seaweed provides sustenance in the ecological system, so does the floating collar represent an essential triumph?

'I'm just breathless,' said one guest, Cecil, who had to be revived with smelling salts. 'Choo Choo has truly triumphed.'

I asked him if he could say that three times fast, but he shyly declined. 'I have a slight lithp,' he explained, hastening to add that many persons found it cute.

Fashion expert Lloyd Pest, who was also present, was less enthusiastic about the floating collar when I approached him for his opinion.

'It is hardly a revisionist, let alone a revolutionary, concept,' he commented to a small group. 'Indeed, the collar is integral to the shirt as a whole, although it lost some popularity in the late 1940s after World War Two.' He paused for a half-hour to collect his thoughts and then continued.

'Whether this departure will be effective in the present situation, given the swing to right-wing conservatism, the highly competitive detergent market and the present trend towards shorter hairstyles, depends a lot on the way Mr Chu markets his shirt. Will the populace be comfortable with a floating collar which, we must admit, is a bold (although, as I say, hardly revisionist) concept? In the final analysis, much depends on the quality of the material used. Indian cotton with bone buttons is only one of my suggestions.'

Mr Pest had much more to say, but everyone had dozed off.

Another fashion expert, Sir Carter Hubris, was entirely pessimistic.

'Keeping the collar folded to the shirt has always been integral to the concept of formality and, if I may say so, the aesthetic unity of the garment itself,' he told me. 'Is this society, powerless in the high-powered fashion industry, really prepared – indeed, competent – to deal with the floating collar? I have my reservations and will be dining at 8.00 p.m. at a small but inexpensive restaurant with a young lady of loose moral character. But this does not mean a shirt with a floating collar is therefore appropriate attire.'

The most negative response, however, undoubtedly came from Chane Leatherette. I later found out that Chane had formerly been Choo Choo's close bedfellow in the fashion industry, but their philosophical differences had led them in different directions. (Choo Choo thinks body-building posters are just darling and can be used as wallpaper; Chane prefers the starker pink handcuffs and thinks all walls should be simply mirrored.)

He had come to the show uninvited and, rather than make a scene, Choo Choo very graciously ignored him. Chane, dressed in a pair of black leather trousers with absolutely no pockets and a pink silk shirt with no collar at all, made a strong statement.

'Pooh,' he said.

When I talked to him, Chane Leatherette insisted that the floating collar was just a passing fad. 'I am just so surprised – indeed, I might even go so far as to say utterly – that Choo Choo would jump on this ostentatious bandwagon,' he said.

He slackened a wrist which had begun to get uncomfortably firm while supplying me with some background into the workings of the fast-paced, highly profitable and cut-throat fashion industry.

'Between you and me and your readers,' he said, 'the poor man hasn't been the same since his best sewer and friend, Rajesh, got married,' said Chane. 'And that new designer he's taken up with –

just a young, inexperienced boy – cannot possibly be expected to perform up to Choo Choo's expectations. Indeed, it wouldn't surprise me at all to discover it was his hand behind this floating collar silliness. It may be art,' he concluded, 'but is it fashionable?'

I did not get a chance to talk to Choo Choo himself until the next day. When I visited him at his country home, he was reclining comfortably with his Siamese cat Fifi, drinking a glass of red wine and watching *As the World Turns*. He seemed entirely unmoved by the uproar his latest innovation had set off.

'People are always shocked by change,' he told me.

I nodded understandingly.

He then made a statement I have never forgotten.

'Style,' he said, 'sets its own trend.'

He went on to explain what he hoped to achieve with the floating collar.

'We have lived with a Third World mentality for too long,' he said. 'We are terrified of being avant-garde. My floating collar rejects any image of backwardness in the modern world. It is, in fact, a development from the upraised collar, typical of raincoats, which is supposed to prevent water dripping down one's back. The upraised collar is designed to prevent wet jockey shorts. My collar,' he said, smiling slightly, 'does not do this. It is filled with helium and has no functional purpose. But it does bring Trinidad fashions in line with the best in New York, Paris and Tokyo.'

Choo Choo also explained that the shirts came in a variety of styles, including extras such as condoms, waterproof jockey shorts and lead weights for ballast. I noticed that he smiled slightly as he mentioned this.

'Just because we're fashionable doesn't mean we can't also be smart,' he said.

I read back Chane Leatherette's comments to him and asked for a response. Choo Choo smiled slightly again.

'Chane is a businessman, I am an artist,' he said. 'I think that is sufficient to explain our differences.'

He went on to explain.

109

'I have a sense of social purpose, of the people whom I am dressing. I believe in a hands-on approach. Chane likes to be more restrained. Frankly, this is not my vision.'

He took a sip from his wineglass and smiled slightly. Curious, I asked him why he always smiled so slightly.

'Haemorrhoids,' he said.

So I wrote my article and carried it in. But it turned out that the weekly, which was called *The Bare Weekly*, had no intention of continuing to run a fashion column. Instead, it was to be replaced by a column on 'Sexual problems and techniques' – a poor decision, I felt, and one which did not cater to the wider tastes of readers. Wolf, however, held that the paper was sold on the basis of its photographs of scantily clad young women. I thought this view foolish, betraying little or no knowledge of human nature, but I said nothing. Wolf was not a very cultured man, and preferred David Rudder, a local composer, to Brahms. Also, he rarely pronounced his 'ths'.

However, my guardian angel was still watching out for me. The fourth factor in my favour was that the weekly newspaper was, at the same time I wrote my article, launching a daily publication. They needed writers and, with my reputation already established from the many pieces I had written to the letters page and my experience in the Information Ministry, I was well-qualified. I was hired to write culture articles, including fashion, naturally.

In truth, I was more comfortable working at the daily than the weekly paper. In fact, the only reason I had even considered working at *Bare* was because I liked the idea of working once a week. But the weekly paper was very much a scandal sheet and, as I have mentioned, carried regular pictures of young women. Many of them posed for their photographs right there in the office. It was only because I knew my presence would uplift *Bare* that I even considered being employed there.

But this daily paper, to be called *The Goodly News*, solved all my problems. It was to be in total contrast to the weekly which

110

supported it. The editor was a woman who had been a leading church-goer, regular columnist and public relations officer for a large toiletries company for many years. She was retired now, but had graciously consented to help launch this new daily paper which was to be devoted to good news, in contrast to the sensationalism and negativity which pervaded the rest of the media. Our goal was to improve society, and my experience at the Information Ministry would be invaluable. I felt I was on a great adventure.

The editor's name, as the reader will have already surmised, was Merle Shoelace. She was a sophisticated woman who, in all the time I knew her, never belched. She had a round face with large spectacles and a short, blue hair-do. Having devoted her life to furthering the cause of women in Trinidad, as well as earning a good salary, she was a leading exemplar in our society. It was a reflection of her social conscience that, although she could have stayed comfortably in retirement doing nothing, she chose to help a weekly newspaper improve its image by publishing a responsible daily. I think she must have helped save several souls by her selfless act. It is interesting to note that she nearly refused the position because the weekly paper published lewd photos of young girls, but she changed her mind when she got her own parking space. I grew to admire Mrs Shoelace tremendously, and she had a great influence on my becoming Paras P.

The paper was successfully launched. The lead story was, as per our policy, an extremely positive one: 'Clean New Daily Hits the Streets', said the front-page headline. My piece on Choo Choo's floating collar was the main article on the feature pages and carried my byline. My only reservation was that Brain might not have approved. Despite his having hit me in the head, I had decided to forgive him, as the Bible instructed. And I still respected the tremendous intellect which had never had a piece published in any magazine since 1945. Brain had explained to me that this was because his writing was too good to be published, but he had no intentions of lowering his standards. I felt he might look at me with contempt because I had been published, but *que sera sera*. I was too taken up with these new challenges to worry about the past. In a very real way, I felt I had found my niche. Even from the start, my moral and spiritual strength subtly influenced the paper's direction while my presence in the newsroom alone, if I may say so, lent a tone.

We had set ourselves a difficult task. In a country like Trinidad at that time, there weren't that many good things happening. And it seemed that fate was conspiring to make our job even more difficult. The very week we began publication, for example, a National Airways aeroplane crashed during take-off, killing everyone on board. This, as you may imagine, was a rather difficult story to write positively. In fact, Mrs Shoelace took the task upon herself and, as you will see from the clipping I have kept, did quite a good job.

A Trinidad aeroplane crashed yesterday afternoon after an explosion on board. Everyone was killed instantly.

However, it has been ascertained that the explosion wasn't because of a bomb or bad maintenance or careless personnel.

Reporters, however, were unable to find out just what the cause of the explosion was.

'We will release details after a full investigation,' said Mr Goodfellow Hypocrates, the airline's manager, in an official statement. 'After all, we wouldn't want citizens to lose faith in our service, would we?' he added with a beautiful and sincere smile.

He did say, however, that no one had suffered, since the aircraft hit the ground only a few seconds after the explosion occurred. He also pointed out that more people might have been killed, but five seats were empty.

The airline will be continuing its operations as usual.

Even in our minor stories, we tried to show events in the best possible light. In the Great Floods of 1982, for example, 16 people lost their lives. Yet we were able to find the silver lining even in that thundercloud. I wrote the following report myself, and consider it one of my most precise pieces of writing. (The discerning reader will detect the Hemingway influence I was then under.)

Patricia Jackson of Tomato Choka Street and her common-law husband, Chotolal Ramesar, were having sex when the flood struck their home.

Because of this, they did not notice the rising waters until it was too late. Both persons drowned. The funeral will take place as soon as the undertaker can get the smiles off their faces.

Our columnists, naturally, tried to look at everything in an incisive but also positive light. We had writing for us Dr Maron Dopak – undoubtedly one of the most intelligent, straightforward and interesting personalities I have ever met. He even had a remarkable physical appearance, since he had skin like soot and eyes like pigeon eggs about to hatch. He shaved his head because, he said, 'I do not share the curse of the sons of Ham.' A well-read and, as I say, erudite person. Dr Dopak was also to prove a significant influence on my life. In tribute to him and so that the reader can understand the clarity of his analytical mind and the honesty of his character, I have reproduced here one of his columns which deals with the same Great Floods and which, I think, said best everything which needed to be said about that event.

Despite the loss of life, we must remember that the floods which hit the capital city yesterday could have had far more serious consequences.

After all, everybody who died or lost their homes was black and ignorant. It was their own fault they built their shacks on sites where the rains could wash them away. And some of the ignorant swine were actually conducting

113

businesses, as though they thought they could be entrepreneurs.

If they had been working for white people, as God intended, they might still be alive today.

Also, on another good note, the Government plans to give people in residential areas monetary compensation. This is a fine display of responsibility since so many wealthy and influential people live in the affected areas.

It also sends a clear message to the ignorant masses who will not get compensation, showing that the Government is serious about creating a well-ordered society where everyone knows his place.

Interestingly, crime presented less of a problem to report. Certainly, a murder happened twice a day, rapes three times every 48 hours, robberies once every hour. But, as we pointed out, that meant 1,499,994 persons in the country weren't murdered and slightly fewer weren't raped, robbed or assaulted.

Our editorials, similarly, were models of public responsibility. Consider, for example, one written by Mrs Shoelace herself on a controversy where government ministers were buying expensive foreign cars while telling citizens to tighten their belts.

We must commend those Government Ministers who have chosen to buy foreign cars costing upward of a quarter-million dollars. In this time of economic stringency, when citizens face steep cost-of-living increases every day, it is heartening to see that Ministers have so much faith in the economy that they are spending valuable foreign exchange in full confidence that the economy will improve.

Indeed, it is certain that once oil prices don't drop, the country will come out of its economic slump. Trinidad has always been lucky in this regard, and we must have faith in our history.

The conspicuous consumption of our Government

Ministers will continue sending a clear and unmistakable message about the committed leadership this country has.

If I have gone into some detail about the daily paper, it is only because it was here that my philosophy and perspective about Correct behaviour truly became honed, shaped and focused. A major influence in this regard, as I have said, was Mrs Shoelace. The other was Dr Dopak.

Dr Dopak and I got along famously from the start. I respected his erudition while he admired me because of my tremendous spiritual authority, intellectual accomplishment and white ancestry. By this I do not mean to imply that Dr Dopak was in any way racist. Indeed, he had a great love for black people, and his habit of referring to them as 'ignorant swine' was meant constructively. We had the following conversation quite early in our relationship, which I recorded. It amply demonstrates, in my opinion, the extraordinary character of the man.

'When I was a small boy,' he told me, 'the other boys used to tell me I was black, stupid and ugly. But I am sure if I kept out of the sun, I wouldn't be as black as I am. In dim light, I can even be mistaken for a white man who's been burnt to death.'

In the intellectual spirit of our conversation, I pointed out that looking at his nose was like looking down a double-barrelled shotgun.

'But my lips make my nose look small,' he said at once. 'It's not my fault that when I was small the bigger boys used to pick me up by my nostrils and make me kiss jep nests,' he pointed out.

I could not argue with this. Dr Dopak was an acute debater.

Dr Dopak had devoted his life to helping improve the lot of his black brethren by shaking them out of their apathy.

'But these Orwellian swine just don't appreciate what I'm trying to do,' he said, 'and I can't figure out why.'

'Maybe you shouldn't use terms like Orwellian swine,' I suggested.

He nodded. 'You may be right. They won't understand the reference. It's the ten thousand illiterates we had at Independence who produced the criminals, bandits and whores of today.'

'Ten thousand?' I said, surprised.

'I didn't just pull that figure out of a hat, you know,' he said, seeming to think I was doubting his statistics. 'Having a doctorate, I have done research proving that not only was it ten thousand illiterates, but it is their children who are the criminals, who were of course produced out of wedlock, proving in turn the pernicious effects of fornication, which I object to because no woman wants to try it with me without payment and a paper bag – where was I?'

'Trying to explain how black people can improve themselves,' I prompted. I was quite fascinated with Dr Dopak's theories and felt I was learning a lot.

'Oh, yes. Black fascists, ignorant mobs of hooligans, uneducated swine, mesmerized by vacuous political nonsense from Communists at the university! I believe strongly in intellectual rigour – I have a doctorate, you know. And there are lots of people in this country who agree with me. Most of them are fair in complexion. Most black people simply cannot understand the facts I am presenting and, as long as that is so, what hope is there?'

Dr Dopak got very depressed when he thought of this.

'I tell the truths that the ignorant black illiterates, the black Marxists at the university and the black politicians don't want to hear. This is how I make my living, because plenty white people support me. This country never had a better economy than when slavery was in force and the illiterate, black, swinish mobs knew their right place. We dismantled that structure and look at the chaos we have today. Is racism wrong when it holds truth?' he asked passionately.

It was a convincing argument. Dr Dopak and I had many more discussions along similar lines. I was quite sorry when his column was stopped because advertisers, including, strangely enough, the white ones, withdrew their support because of his ideas.

116

Still, his influence remained with me and I understood that my mission in life was to improve the attitudes of those who did not understand the importance of an ordered, prosperous society. More and more I was beginning to understand the true nature of Correctness.

My career in journalism, short as it was, also carried me into spheres I might not otherwise have entered. It was the prejudice I discovered in some of these spheres which aroused my humanitarian concern for the suffering masses. To this day, when I think about the starving millions in Africa, I often have to refuse a second helping of custard pie. And, when the famine was taking place in Ethiopia, the scenes so upset me that I actually turned off the television until *Dynasty* started.

My first experience of such prejudice occurred when I attended the KFC Club's first Annual Poetry Day in honour of Derek Walcott. This was just after he had been accepted at Boston University and people in Trinidad realized he had a reputation.

I had got quite excited when Mrs Shoelace passed on her beautifully engraved invitation. She was unable to attend because of an engagement with her hairdresser to restore the blue in her hair. I was quite happy about this, thinking I would be able to gorge myself on free fried chicken. But KFC, I found out too late, stands for Knights of the First Colony.

With much muttering of dire imprecations, therefore – when one has set one's mind on eating fried chicken and finds one must listen to poetry instead, one's mood naturally becomes fowl – I got out my waistcoat, my book of quotations and lost ten pounds in two days. (This is done by drinking only senna tea at meals and eating nothing but grapefruits. It is a quite drastic method and entails a lot of fainting, but very soon one has the triumph of being able to look in the mirror and see 'a needy, hollow ey'd, sharp-looking wretch'.)

When I presented myself at precisely 7.30 p.m. at the exclusive Country Club, the two elderly gentlemen at the door, who undoubtedly entertained fond memories of Queen Victoria, seemed to concur. As they scanned my invitation, I distinctly heard one mutter into the hearing-trumpet of his companion, 'Yon'd reporter has a lean and hungry look; he thinks too much; such men are dangerous.'

While I appreciated the tribute to both my brain and my waistline, I realized I should avoid contention.

'But thought's the slave of life, and life time's fool,' I suggested and, reluctantly I thought, they let me pass.

As I entered the great hall, I realized that I was even more out of place than I had realized. Being half-white, I had never experienced prejudice or, if I did, I dismissed it as mere jealousy. But, in that exclusive place, I could have been a pure kaffir. It was a learning experience and, as most such experiences are, quite upsetting.

Nonetheless, these were people of breeding and betrayed no rancour. I was warmly welcomed by the hosts, who had been specially imported from England for the occasion: Lord Knowsley Rightpaddle Tolpuddle, who had distinguished himself during the civil disobedience in India, and his lovely wife who, at 82, didn't seem a day under 80. To my delight, my great friend Dr Maron Dopak was there. He had arrived ten minutes before me and was still prostrating himself before Lord Tolpuddle.

Mindful that I was working, I got a drink and a plate of hors d'œuvres and moved around the crowd. As I had expected in such a distinguished gathering, the conversation ranged widely over sports, politics and, of course, poetry.

'What the Americans fail to realize is that Britain still rules the waves,' said one noble-looking gentleman who clearly knew what he was talking about. 'Mr Reagan has quite an aggressive foreign policy, but one merely has to look at the Queen, the natural poise, the grace of her wrist and the perfect angle at which she holds her hand, to see her mastery.'

In another part of the room, a prosperous looking blond man with a strange accent said, 'There's good game here. In my country, the buggers are so fast that it's difficult to pot them even with a high-powered rifle. I think we need to feed them less.'

It was not too long before the main part of the function commenced. And, after we had dinner, extracts from Walcott's works were read out loud by Trevor 'Tadpole' Tringdiddle, the well-known playwright and cross-dresser.

'I have a complete collection of Walcott,' the fair lady seated next to me said. 'I had it imported the very week he started work in Boston.'

'What do you think of *Another Life*?' I asked.

'Oh, it's my favorite soap!' she said.

'I meant Walcott's book,' I said.

'Oh,' she said. 'Yes, I have it in hardcover.'

The evening was so uplifting that I didn't leave until five minutes later, hiding an extra dessert under my coat. As I passed the two old gentlemen at the door, for spite I said, 'How weary, stale, flat and unprofitable seem to me all the uses of this world.'

This, of course, totally outraged them.

'He must be a Socialist,' I heard one of them say accusingly as I went out.

I will admit, though, that this was just pique. My experience with the KFC Club gave me cause to ponder long and hard. Previously, I had looked upon my fair skin as an advantage. Now I saw that, when one encountered people with even fairer skin, one's complexion made little difference. What was important, I realized, was attitude. After all, even Dr Dopak, because they recognized intellectual worth, was welcomed in that fair throng. I had fallen into the same error of those persons in my younger days who saw just my pimples and not the smooth complexion below them.

For perhaps the first time in my life, I found myself truly empathizing with those who went through life dark-skinned and suffered calumny because of this. Was it fair? I thought. The answer, obviously, was no.

I had tried to fool myself that I was not truly one of the coloured peoples of the world. But Dr Dopak had showed me this was not the right attitude.

'I am black,' he once admitted to me. 'But I regret it and so am able to rise above it.'

It was then I got an inkling of my true purpose in life. And then the incident which led to my being fired from *The Goodly News* occurred. This was the final lesson which put all the pieces in place for me and launched the name of Paras P.

Briefly, what happened was this. I had by this time established a fairly wide network of contacts in both the public and private sector. It was one of my sources from the Health Ministry who brought me the following story. It sounded plausible and I had no reason to doubt my source. He even provided the memos, though perhaps the pink colour of the paper they were written on should have sounded a warning. But he assured me the foreign wire services would be carrying the exact story the following day. So I felt I was on solid ground.

More to the point, Mrs Shoelace agreed with me. She asked me if I had documentation and quotes. I said yes. I remember her exact words quite clearly and also have them on tape. My pocket recorder, as you realize, was hardly ever off.

'It's late, we don't have a lead story and sales yesterday were terrible,' she said. 'Let's go with it.'

I still hold that there was a lot of truth in my story. Dr Dopak, whom I contacted for a comment, agreed with me. My own feeling is that the World Health Organization got wind of our exclusive in Trinidad and did a quick cover-up. In fact, I argued this at the time, but failed to convince the management. But what could you expect of a newspaper which published semi-nude photos of young women? (For the daily had also begun doing this to increase sales. Mrs Shoelace, in fact, nearly resigned over the issue but was offered a lunch allowance and had to stay on.)

Here, then, is the story.

A 1983 study on skin cancer in Caribbean countries, sponsored by the World Health Organization (WHO), was really designed to reduce the number of dark-skinned people in the Caribbean population.

Internal memos between WHO directors, several scientists and a major sunblock manufacturer were leaked to this paper earlier this week. The memos reveal that statistics linking cancer rates to exposure to the sun are entirely fabricated.

The project, if initially successful in the Caribbean, was to be extended to India and eventually Africa. By convincing people that exposure to the sun caused cancer, wrinkling, premature aging and sterility, it was hoped that individuals would be persuaded to stay out of the sun and so get lighter complexions.

One WHO director defended the rationale behind the project. 'The prejudice against dark-skinned people is real,' he said. 'If within three generations WHO could have significantly lightened the complexions of most of the world's peoples, we would also have eradicated the bigotry which prevents world peace and economic stability.'

Rumours of this report have already caused stock markets to react negatively, with shares in major sunblock companies dropping an average of five points. However, sales of bathing suits and tanning lotion reportedly increased.

Actor Sidney Poitier is reportedly to star in a movie about the scandal called *White Men Can't Tan*. 'This will be the most powerful film ever on the question of historical and contemporary racism,' he said in an official statement. 'And if I don't get an Oscar next year it will prove the Academy is prejudiced against black movie stars.'

Locally, well-known academic Dr Maron Dopak commented, 'It is a tragedy that irrational, ignorant prejudices should have stopped such a fine idea from being implemented.'

When the other media, undoubtedly motivated by craven fear of competition, carried out their own investigation and 'proved' this report false, I was handed my notice.

It did not surprise me. All great men have suffered. But I now saw my path clearly before me. A grassy one, with flowers and brickwork on the side and a dazzling light at the end of a tunnel. I've never smoked marijuana since then, at least not inhaling when I did so. But I was very depressed at the time. However, I should have had faith for, as with children and dumb animals, there is a power which looks after good men.

Chapter Seven

But could youth last, and love still breed;
Had joys no date, nor age no need;
Then those delights my mind might move
To live with thee and be thy love.

From 'The Nymph's Reply to the
Shepherd' by Sir Walter Raleigh

I had not, until this point in my life, been too concerned with love.
I had my memories of Selina, doomed though that relationship
had been. Also, like all great men, I had been too busy making my
name in the world to think about the softer emotions. But my
burgeoning philosophy of Correctness gnawed at me without my
being aware of it. Deep within myself, I understood that a man of
my age should be married and raising a family. Otherwise, people
started wondering if he was homosexual.

Someone as masculine as myself did not need to worry about
this, but I was aware of an emptiness in my life, a hollowness in
the centre of my being. I tried eating five meals a day, but this
proved only a palliative for what truly ailed me. Only after
implementing my senna tea diet and losing my job did I understand
that this emptiness within me had nothing to do with lamb chops,
pasta and baked potatoes.

Now that this crisis had been precipitated in my affairs, I realized
that what my life needed was True Love. Preferably with inherited
wealth. But this, I also realized, was not going to be easy to find.

My name, at this stage in my life, was still Paras Parmanandan-singh. And, since I have resolved to be entirely honest in giving this account of my life, I must now admit that my middle name was Karamdass.

How, you may ask, did this affect me? The unpleasant truth is that modern Western society had not catered for Paras Karamdass Parmanandansingh. I first knew this when, at the tender age of ten, I had to fill out an official form.

That was in primary school, for the Common Entrance Examination. Needless to say, the exam was nearly done by the time I finished. Fortunately, it was multiple choice and I was able to shade quickly.

But, for my entire life, filling out forms had always been a nightmare. There was never enough space and, at banks, super-markets, credit unions and gas stations, people in the line behind me always steupsed at being kept waiting. Naturally, this made me feel alienated from my society. The only silver lining was that I never faced this trauma in government offices, where people expect to be kept waiting. In fact, in my later political career, I lobbied assiduously against efficiency in the public service, know-ing it would militate against people with names as long as mine. It was the only ethnic position I ever took up.

But it was also my name, I felt, which accounted for my romantic failure. After all, I was a 'good catch', as women put it. I had a public image, dressed with excellent taste, I was extremely spiritual, conversed well about my dreams, desires and ambitions, had good table manners, a father who owned land, never tanned and was toilet-trained from an early age. I also made a pretty toothsome egg salad. And yet most of the women I met seemed not to have a passion for egg salad. I could not understand it.

The only logical barrier, I came to realize, had to be my name. Most women understandably would think twice before changing their name to Parmanandansingh. Besides the length, you never knew how the audience in church might react.

Some people might argue about this. 'What's in a name?' Juliet

124

once asked. But would the fire of passion have raged in her heart if Romeo had been christened Ebenezer? Would she have been out on her balcony crying, 'O Ebenezer, Ebenezer! wherefore art thou, Ebenezer?' I *don't* think so.

So, very quietly and without much fuss, I changed my name to Paras Parman. Extremist, I know, but I have never been a man to do anything by half-measures. I must hasten to explain that the public reasons I offered later for becoming Paras P., when I became known, as the media dubbed me, as the 'Father of Correctness', are not invalid. But, as with every great man, there was the public image and the private persona – the former known to the multitudes, as I like to call my fans, the latter known only to a privileged few, as I like to call my family and friends.

Adding to my difficulties, though, were the high standards I had set for myself. In the ordinary run of things, it was difficult for a man like myself to find a suitable mate. Prince Charles, just a few years previously, had been expressing similar difficulties. I wanted a woman who was intelligent, beautiful, spiritual, shaved and with her own money.

It was not that I was mercenary. In fact, I was quite willing to compromise on this matter of money. I did not insist on inherited wealth, if my intended wife had a steady income. But the reader must understand that I was at a stage in my life where I was intensely concerned about spiritual matters. And I knew that, while you could live on love alone, you definitely had to skip lunch sometimes. This I was unwilling to do. Not, I must repeat, because I was in any way mercenary. But even Mahatma Gandhi, whom I was coming to resemble, would have admitted that it is difficult to concentrate on the nature of God when your stomach is rumbling. That's why Muslims worship Allah so loudly, often using microphones. It's not that they think Allah is deaf. In fact, the Qu'ran says that Allah hears everything, sees everything, though, as far as I know, Oprah Winfrey is no relation. But nobody who isn't anorexic fasts more than Muslims – a habit they acquired in the early days of their religion, when it was called starving. For several times of the year, they fast between sunrise and sunset, and the noise of all those grumbling stomachs would drown out their prayers if they didn't yell them out.

The point is, I knew that, for both my emotional and spiritual health, I needed the kind of relationship which is so rare nowadays: one based on mutual love, respect and trust – the kind of relationship with a joint chequing account.

In a multi-ethnic society like Trinidad, there were many paths to God I could have chosen. My upbringing had not predisposed me to any particular one, although, for reasons I have already outlined, I could not be a Muslim. My ancestral religion, Hinduism, had its good points, but I didn't like repeating myself.

For these reasons, among others, I turned to Christianity. But now I had the problem of choosing among all the different sects.

Small churches, which attracted mostly the lower classes, were out of the question. Most persons of East Indian ancestry who had converted to Christianity had gone to the Presbyterian Church. But after attending one sermon, I realized I would not be able to adhere to this branch of Christianity. The reverend spoke in an accent I knew I could never acquire, and nearly all the men in the congregation wore shirtjacs. I had a conviction – not exactly a revelation, but very close – that God would not approve my joining a church whose members wore shirtjacs.

I briefly considered favouring the Anglican Church with my presence. But I wondered if one could one depend on a church founded by a king with eight wives. Or on one in which in Trinidad, a leading priest had fled back to Scotland after converting several small boys to homosexual practices. The Anglican Church had brought charges against several newspaper editors for reporting that story. Besides all this, though, I doubted I would find a suitable wife in a church where so many of the women wore horn-rimmed spectacles with – and this is the gospel truth – white stockings.

And so I turned to Catholicism. I realized that the Catholic Church was closer to God than any other religion. They had the

126

best churches, really fashionable robes and a pretty good dental plan. Clearly, God had showered his blessings upon them.

Besides this, though, I had never forgotten Father Royd. I remembered well his inner strength, intensity, confidence and controlled calm. I wanted to be like him.

Last but not least, I also figured that my chances of finding a truly spiritual woman with a steady income were higher here than in any other religion. Iran had oil, but it didn't have the financial clout of the Vatican.

So my long-held interest in Christianity finally became official. I converted, bought an entirely new wardrobe and stopped masturbating. Within a very short time, I became a public relations officer for the West Indian Council of Churches and a church usher. Once again, my intellectual prowess, and ability to dress well, stood me in good stead. I am certain that, had I not made my last name more manageable, and written my first name in such a way that it looked like 'Paris', I would not have advanced so rapidly. And, of course, the religious leaders recognized my spiritual gifts.

However, I did not have any intention of becoming a priest, though you met a lot of women that way and, not infrequently, heard everything about their sex lives. There was no doubt priesthood was an interesting career, but I wanted something more. I would have been satisfied being a PR officer only but, as an usher, I met as many women as any priest. By positioning myself strategically during the church service, I could also press their hands during the blessing. 'Peace unto you,' I would quote, while my eyes emphasized the 'unto'. Mostly, the woman would blush prettily, or drop her eyes or, in a spirit certainly not in keeping with the holy mood, even pull back her hand sharply. But never could I meet that special someone whose hand was as sweaty as my own. (What better test of mutual passion could there be?)

As I moved from church to church, I became more involved in church activities than even the priests. I was in on retreats, discussion groups, counselling sessions, soup kitchens, visits to the

127

sick and poor, and so on. Especially when refreshments were served. I particularly liked visiting the poor and sick, because, if you timed it right, you would generally get dinner. In those impecunious days, every little bit helped, and I in my turn gave these deprived people spiritual solace, usually before dessert.

So my life was very busy When I was not ushering, I was busy answering letters to the Pope who, though infallible, apparently couldn't keep up with his mail. Some of the letters I was able to answer myself, some I had to pass on to Father Torval, head of WICC, for approval. I have included here a fairly select sample of the type of mail I received so the reader may understand the difficulty of my task, and the influence on people's lives I wielded even then.

Dear Holy Father

Thank you for sending your official list of new sins as requested. However, we thought the rates for absolution a little steep, and were wondering if there was a special discount for multiple applications. As you know, in my clients' line of work, it is in any case difficult to commit one sin without committing several others. And this, I assure you, weighs very heavily on their consciences.

We would greatly appreciate, therefore, a bulk discount for the sins of making profits through embezzlements, tax fraud, forging cheques or invoices and paying unfair salaries.

We would also appreciate it if you would let us know the atonements, in terms of cash contributions and Hail Marys, which will be needed for these transgressions. For accounting purposes, however, please itemize each sin separately. Please say if, given these new listings, additional visits to the confessional are required.

We will continue to pay the normal rates, plus inflation, for murder, greed and covetousness.

Very sincerely yours,

Mario Pedro Corleone MBA

This one I passed on to Father Torval, who nodded and said, 'We've been needing a new chalice for the vestry.'

Other letters, like the following one, dealt with church policy. The Vatican liked to know what the faithful were thinking.

Dear Holy Father
        Heartiest congratulations on your recent pronouncement that the Church has no power to ordain women as priests. It is good to see you are standing up for tradition, though I am still a little upset over the pronouncement about Galileo. The Church cannot shift and chop at every little wind. Like Peter, we must remain a rock. My wife tried to argue with me, saying the Church can alter its teaching on anything not specified in the Bible, but after three beatings she learned to stop blaspheming. I don't know where women are getting all these ideas from. I do hope, however, that the Church isn't going to apologize to Jews. This admission that the Church can be wrong would seriously undermine her authority. Besides, they killed Christ, didn't they?
                                Yours truly
                                Sterling Manley

One often received personal letters from women.

Dear Holy Father
        I have been a devout Catholic for 53 years and I am so gladdened by the recent ruling by the Holy Father that it is no sin to seek pleasure in sex but that we should be moderate.

        I have been married for 34 years and I have never had the slightest pleasure out of sex. My husband did seek sexual pleasure, however, and I did my duty by him as a good wife should. I confess that once, in the summer of 1962, I nearly had an orgasm. Luckily, the feeling passed. But I can assure you, Holy Father, that my husband never got any more enjoyment out of sex with me than the Good Lord intended.

For some reason, though, he started seeking sex with other women in the second year of our marriage. But I stayed with him because I know divorce is wrong, wrong, wrong.

Even so, my husband is basically a good Catholic, and has never worn a condom. Thus, we have nine children, and it would have been thirteen if I hadn't had four miscarriages. And there would certainly have been even more if I had got any pleasure in sex or kept my figure. Truly, Holy Father, the Church is wise.

My example has persuaded my husband to finally seek the faith, though, and he doesn't even try to have sex with me anymore. In fact, I am glad to say he has become a most attentive father, and spends a lot more time with the children, especially the twins, Patsy and Paula, who have just turned sixteen. Patsy, I notice, has begun to get fat. Could you say a prayer for her?

Yours faithfully,
Domini Martinez

To this I gave a standard reply, commending her for her steadfast faith and promising a prayer for her fat daughter. Some letters, such as the following, were more mysterious.

Dear Holy Father

My name is Paul. I earn my living as a fisherman. My ancestors came from Jerusalem.

Obviously, I should be Pope. I would like to take up the position as soon as possible.

Yours faithfully,
Paul Poisson

I first thought of passing this on to Father Torval, but a little reflection showed me a form answer would suffice. I wrote Mr

Poisson informing him that the post was already filled but thanks for his interest and we would keep his application on file.

Other letters showed how much good work the WICC, in which I played so integral a part, was doing in the region.

Dear Holy Father

Our recent conference on 'Love, Life and the Family' here in the Caribbean was a notable success. Through prayer and lots of singing, we managed to make the forces of evil retreat from this blessed land.

On the theme of Life, we told all those so-called 'pro-choice' people that they were nothing but filthy murderers. We went on television and told the public how 60 years ago family planning was only a plan to stop black people from breeding. Our stance has always worked, since poor black people breed like rabbits. Those who are better off have smaller families, proving that wealthy people are materialistic and lack spiritual conviction.

On the theme of Family, we showed how disgusting and unnatural homosexuality is and did our best to ensure normal people would be entirely disgusted with the practices of these unnatural and depraved persons. We are sure everybody in the Caribbean who attended our conference will shun homosexuals from now on. This will prevent homosexuality from spreading and help preserve morality.

Unfortunately, the conference lasted only one week and we weren't able to get around to Love. But we think you will agree, Holy Father, that two out of three isn't bad.

Faithfully yours,
Barnabas Richwright

I wrote back to Mr Richwright commending him on his good work.

This, I hope, gives you some idea of the type of work I did in that period of my life and how it influenced my later mission as

131

Paras P. But the major influence to shape my life in that period was undoubtedly my first wife – Gloria Neehall.

Gloria was entirely unlike the first great love of my life, Selina. She had a small nose, long hair and was brown-skinned. Not, you would think, the kind of woman who would attract me. And you would be right because, when she came into church, I entirely overlooked her. It was, in fact, *she* who placed herself next to *me* for the exchange of blessings. This was the first experience I had of Gloria's strong will.

It was a warm, still evening at Mass. I was, at the time, concentrating my attention on a tall girl with coffee-coloured skin and the kind of legs which would undoubtedly have made a weaker man wonder what it would be like to have them wrapped around his neck. I, however, was interested only in her character and monthly income.

And then Gloria took my hand. I did not even look at her until I realized our palms were adhering like sticking plaster because of the sweat. And, as I noticed her for the first time, I realized it was not merely the heat of the evening which caused this.

She gazed me straight in the eyes and said, 'You have Scottish or English or French ancestry, don't you?'

'My mother was Canadian,' I said frankly. I had never been one to deny my heritage.

A glazed look came into Gloria's eyes.

'I could tell. I can usually tell,' she said.

'She died when I was very young,' I said.

'But her spirit remains with you.'

'Like the Holy Ghost,' I agreed.

At that moment we realized we were still holding hands, and released our grip with smiles of embarrassment and a wet, sucking sound. Luckily, the people near us seemed only to think I had belched. I was greatly relieved at this, for I would not have liked anyone saying I had been courting in church. As Aristotle once put it, 'Only when a thing is expressed does it become real to the

132

mind, as apart from the senses, causing severe embarrassment.' I believe that he had, at the time, been caught in the sauna with a young Greek soldier.

I shall pass lightly over my courtship of Gloria, which took a month. (Despite my family history, I thought I should proceed slowly.) Suffice to say that Gloria proved to have much of what I desired in a woman. She was spiritual, intelligent, listened well and was an accountant with a reputable firm in the city.

I do not imply she was perfect. She spoke, like most Trinidadians, with a distinct Trinidadian accent. She liked having things her own way and her calves were on the slim side. Also, though she stayed out of the sun, she remained as brown as a nut. But I was capable of compromise, except in regard to my principles.

In fact, one of the things I most admired about Gloria, and which persuaded me to ask her to do me the honour of becoming my wife, was her highly developed ethical sense.

'There are so few fair men in this country,' she told me one night, snuggling her head against my chest.

'I have always believed in fairness,' I told her.

'That's one of the reasons I love you,' she said. 'Because you're such a fair man. We could have lovely children, who would have status in society.'

'We would certainly bring them up with a sense of fair play,' I agreed. Nothing, I knew, redeemeth a man more than good character.

'They would be born so,' she answered, showing a touching faith in God and our genes. 'They wouldn't be like me.' A touch of bitterness came into her tone. 'All my sisters are fair. I was always the black one in the family,' she said, leaving out the word 'sheep' in her emotion.

'But you are fair,' I said truthfully, because she had never treated me unjustly in all the time we had been dating. When we had food in a Chinese restaurant, she shared the portions equally and often

133

insisted on paying. (Of course, I always did the Correct thing and paid half.)

She looked at me with shining eyes. 'No, I am not. But it nice of you to say so.'

And, argue though I might, I could not convince her that she was the fairest woman I knew. But this modesty only endeared me to her all the more.

It seemed a match made in Heaven. Little did I know the problems that were to beset us almost from day one.

In the wisdom of my advanced years, I have often wondered if marriage is indeed a covenant. It seems to me that some mistake of translation or interpretation may have occurred in the Bible, and marriage is really a curse. After all, God must have married Adam and Eve before driving them out of the Garden of Eden since He wouldn't have let them live in sin. Maybe, therefore, making them man and wife was their real punishment, and it has been passed on ever since.

Don't misunderstand me. I know marriage is a holy state. But it is also a law of God that everyone who struggles spiritually also has to undergo untold suffering. Coincidence? I think not. Solomon, for example, had great wisdom and many wives. But consider the amount of nagging he must have endured to attain such wisdom!

The reader must not think that my first marriage left me bitter. 'Thoughtful', perhaps, would be the more appropriate adjective. My diary records that period in pitiless detail and, I must say, some pretty fluid prose.

Despite its drawbacks, I admit there are many advantages to marriage. For one thing, you no longer have to pay for sex. And women no longer have to spend as much money on clothes and make-up. This is really why two can live as cheaply as one, especially if they use the same toothbrush.

The first year of our marriage was perfectly blissful. We lived together in deep spirituality, growing closer to God daily. After we felt our intimacy was as perfect as it could be, we decided to have sex. Not often, because we couldn't afford to have children yet and, being Catholic, we couldn't use contraceptives. Also, we wanted to have our own house to raise our children in.

After three years, and the timely death of Gloria's father, we had enough money to take a loan. Now, in debt for the rest of my natural life, I felt truly established in society. I felt I could ask for nothing more. I had a wife, a house, an important job, a personal relationship with God who, if He had a private telephone number would, I was certain, have given it to me. Life was perfect.

And then my hairline started to recede.

This had not bothered me previously. The recession, as I have mentioned, merely gave me a high forehead and made me look intelligent without all the bother of plastic surgery. But between an intellectual appearance and a bald one there is, I discovered, all too thin a line.

The recession of my hairline put great stress on our marriage. I could not admit to Gloria that I was losing my hair. For her to wake up one morning and discover that she had married a bald man would, I felt, be too great a shock for her sensitive nature. Gloria was, I knew, an intensely loyal woman and to be sleeping with a man who did not look like the man she married could, I felt, make her feel all the guilt of an adulteress.

So, for the first time in our marriage, I deceived my wife. Taking some money out of our joint account, I bought a toupée – and did not tell her.

But this dishonesty, for all that it was in a good cause, took its toll. Gloria was a social person, and enjoyed nothing more than going to church bazaars. But, wearing a toupée, I naturally became extremely nervous about going out anywhere where there might be a strong wind. Even in a restaurant, if I saw a fat man ordering beans, I would at once get up and insist we leave.

Gloria was also very affectionate, and when I insisted she stop gripping my hair during intimate moments, she was quite hurt.

135

'I'll buy some new handcuffs,' I said, trying to comfort her. She did not smile. 'And a whip,' I said. She cheered up then, but I knew our relationship had lost something. And, once, when I saw her breaking eggs, I completely lost my temper.

Not that the eventual failure of my marriage was entirely my fault. Almost as soon as we moved into our new house, I discovered fundamental philosophical differences between us. The issue of hanging, for example, became a burning bone of contention between us.

In a way, perhaps neither of us were to blame. We lived in a developing nation where, although hanging was legal, it was never carried out. Therefore, citizens were in a quandary: was hanging all right or not?

I adopted the Christian view and opposed it. And, naturally, I had always assumed Gloria did so, too. Picture my shock, therefore, as we sat one quiet evening in the porch, when she said, 'Some hanging plants would look nice out here.'

I actually felt myself turn pale, but I was too shocked to appreciate it. I looked up at the brand new, polished teak boards of the roof and said, 'You want to put *hooks* into the brand-new, polished teak boards of our new house?'

'Is just wood,' she answered thoughtlessly, like a woman.

I drew a deep breath and brought all my eloquence to bear. 'Just wood, you say? Is the Taj Mahal, then, just a tomb? Is the Grand Canyon just a hole in the ground? Is Derek Walcott just a poet West Indian academics boast they know personally?'

Gloria's reply, like a serpent's tooth, revealed how sharp a woman's tongue can be. 'Yes,' she said.

We argued long and bitterly that evening. Finally, more for the sake of peace than anything else, and because I didn't want to sleep on the living-room couch, I gave in. But I was not happy and, after she had put up her plants, I found myself wincing every time they creaked in the wind. And every time I winced, Gloria steupsed. Our marriage, I realized, was degenerating.

One day I reached home to find she had put up Japanese prints

136

on thin chains in the living-room. They were to me an unbearable reminder of mortality, like too much starch in your jockey shorts. Still, I controlled myself.

'Doesn't the room look lovely?' she said.

'Gloria,' I said, very gently, 'I think you should analyse carefully this urge you have to hang things. You probably think you can take it or leave it alone. But are you truly in control?'

'Oh, you just being silly,' she said, fingering her earlobes. Only then, with dawning horror, did I see that she was wearing hanging earrings.

The strain began to tell on me. I started at sudden noises, and began notching my belt two holes deeper. When I looked into the mirror I saw an awful, haunted image. If the Ancient Mariner had come along in that period, he would have clapped me on the back at once, recognizing a kindred spirit.

Then came the day Gloria said she wanted to hang some paintings on the wall. It was then I put my foot down.

'I will not,' I said, 'have paintings hanging on my wall.'

'But it will make the place look so much better,' Gloria said.

'In order to hang paintings, you must drive nails. It was that kind of impulse which put Christ on the cross. I will not have my walls defaced.'

'I want the paintings,' she said, deaf to all reason.

'Well, you can't have them,' I said cleverly.

Well, Gloria argued long and loud. But I stood firm, except when she kicked me in the shins. Then I hopped about and, I regret to say, used bad language. But the paintings never did go up.

I had won that round, but other issues, both public and personal, came to bedevil us. There was, for example, the matter of water.

In our Third World country, the supply of this basic commodity was quite irregular. Although we had a tank, we had to be careful to use our water sparingly. But our priorities, I discovered, were entirely different. Gloria was quite willing that I wear my old clothes while my newer and more fashionable wear was thrown into the hamper until water came.

'If we wash clothes every week, we won't have water to bathe,' she said.

This lack of logic irritated me.

'Why do you think we have cologne?' I pointed out.

She looked at me with an astonished expression.

'You've got to be clean,' she said, as if announcing the law of gravity.

'A sponge bath will do and uses very little water,' I explained patiently, 'and cologne makes everyone smell alike. But if I'm not properly dressed, *everyone* can see.'

But, despite the force of my argument, Gloria still refused to wash and, being a man, I could not of course wash my own clothes. (It is the abandonment of such old-fashioned standards which has led to the spread of homosexuality in these times. In my own small way, I refused to contribute to this trend.)

Even so, I feel our marriage might have survived. Philosophical differences between men and women can always be overcome or, indeed, ignored entirely, once you're having good sex. But, since her paintings didn't go up, Gloria determined nothing else would either, and began withholding her favours from me. She said it was because my feet smelled. I offered to wear shoes and socks to bed, but she refused.

It was then that suspicion flared briefly in me, but I dismissed the thought as unlikely and, indeed, unworthy. But the fact remains that I was talking about my best leather shoes and black nylon stretch socks.

And then, in this tense period, when it needed just a spark to ignite the powder-keg our marriage had become, Gloria caught me in the bathroom without my toupée.

I was so mortified, the only thing I could think to do was to pretend to be someone else.

'Hello,' I said, trying to change my voice, 'I's one of Paras's friends. He tell me I could use the bathroom.'

138

'Sure, go right ahead,' Gloria replied calmly, and stepped out.

I almost collapsed with the relief at having pulled off the charade. But not too many days passed before darker thoughts intruded. Gloria, I felt, had treated the presence of a stranger in our bathroom with unnatural aplomb. And she had not even asked my 'friend' where Paras was.

Would any decent woman have been so calm?

These thoughts grew on me. And twice after that, she caught me without my hair-piece, and always she accepted my story about being a friend of Paras who just had free run of the house. One of those times was in the bedroom and I was half-naked. Yet Gloria just nodded and smiled.

It was not too long before my suspicions became too great to contain. I accused her of having an affair with a beady-eyed, bald man right in our home.

She denied it, of course. She even argued that she knew it was me all along and had just played along to avoid embarrassing me. I realized then that this woman not only considered me a fool, but a gullible fool.

We separated at once and were divorced within three months.

Chapter Eight

All the world's a stage,
And all the men and women merely players:
They have their exits and their entrances;
And one man in his time plays many parts.

> From *As You Like It* by William
> Shakespeare

I need scarcely say that my decision to get a divorce was not an easy one. It meant that I would have to leave the Church, which didn't approve of divorce or unmarried people above 30.

Divorce also meant giving up my new house. It meant – obviously – giving up my relatively new wife. It even meant giving up my favourite frying pan which I used to make my breakfast pancakes. It was when this sunk in that I truly felt the sharp bitterness of loss. I might have pancakes in the future, but they would not be the same. That is how life is. We become accustomed to our routines and assume they will never change. And what happens? We wake up one morning to find ourselves making pancakes in a strange frying pan. Bitter, bitter.

I think, were it not for this, I could even have found it within me to forgive Gloria. Even when she called me a 'short, fat, bald, paranoid delusional egomaniac', I instinctively knew that she loved me still.

I did not want to hurt her. A divorce is always harder on a woman than a man, unless the woman throws dishes and has a good aim. A divorced woman has a stigma which brings men around like male dogs. Whereas a single man has trouble just getting a date to go to the cinema. Luckily, there are organizations which help divorced men get over the trauma, and the escort service I contacted proved quite efficient.

We sold the house and split the proceeds. Gloria remarried a year later. I saw the wedding photo in the papers. The groom wore a fine hair-piece, and I could barely tell it from the real thing.

Meanwhile, I had gotten on with my life. I stayed on as PR officer tying up loose ends, carrying on routine duties, preparing to hand over, until they finally had to call in security. Father Torval had informed me several months previously that as a PR person I was now a bad advertisement and, as a man, liable to fornicate. He assured me this was not his personal view but a matter of principle.

'I know you wouldn't go with women, Paris,' he said.

'Of course not,' I assured him.

'And certainly not with men,' he said, laughing.

'God, no Father, you can rest assured on *that*,' I said, also chuckling.

Father Torval stopped laughing. 'I'm sorry I can't help you, then,' he said.

'That's all right,' I said, touched by his commiseration.

I felt I had lost everything. I certainly couldn't find my car keys. Then I remembered: Gloria had got the car in the settlement. The law, I felt, was an ass. A woman can more easily obtain transport than a man, especially if she is wearing a low-cut blouse. Yet the court had given her the car. What kind of legal system, I wondered gloomily, did we have?

This put my thoughts on another path. It was, in a sense, the system which had intruded into my marriage to Gloria. We were in an economic recession. It had been proven that women's hemlines rose as the economy improved, and fell as the economy worsened. And it was as if a bright light burst in my brain: *might not the same thing apply to hairlines*? I had never had a more

141

stunning revelation, except when Gloria slapped me really hard the first time she wore her leather suit. (As an intellectual, I felt obliged to try all methods of mental development.) As for the issue of hanging, if a pusillanimous bureaucracy had made up its mind, Gloria and I might never have argued about it.

I was a man devoted to Correct Behaviour. But I realized now I had a larger task – to ensure that the systems which shaped the world were also Correct. Just as God had sacrificed His son on the Cross, so had He sacrificed me on the altar of marriage. The Lord, I saw, had a larger Plan for me. I was being nudged in a certain direction. It was a marvellous and uplifting revelation, personally to feel the Elbow of God.

What had broken my marriage was larger than myself or Gloria. In a word, it was politics. And now, having no job, no prospects for any, and no special skills, I resolved to become a politician. I knew I had found my true niche.

I took it as a personal sign from God when several members of parliament resigned after the Jamette Uprising of 27 July, when it was revealed several MPs regularly visited prostitutes. (I, I admit, had also paid for sex, but never with a prostitute and, in any case, I was not an MP. Nor was it that I was a lewd or even lustful person. It was only that, at the time, my ambition was to be as noted a writer as V.S. Naipaul.)

Readers may remember that infamous incident, when the Jamettes Inc. invaded Parliament one Friday evening, demanding monies owed to them by MPs for services rendered. The jamettes had always been content to work on a pay-when-you-come system. But as many MPs suffered from impotence, this worked to the jamettes' disadvantage. Then Al Bu Cracker, a former Muslim and later professional pimp, decided to organize the prostitutes into a credit union league. The league gained membership rapidly, particularly from men who suffered from premature ejaculation.

Those MPs who were regular customers also joined the league. But it was not too long before they had run up large tabs, and then came the day when 114 prostitutes invaded parliament and the country's three television stations, waving these tabs for all to see.

Five politicians, three from government and two from the opposition, resigned. One minister, though named, refused to resign, claiming he was an innocent bystander. This minister even had videotape proving he never actually touched the jamatte posing for him.

Since God had cleared the way of sinners, I felt obligated to apply as a candidate in the by-elections which now had to be held.

I had no fixed allegiances and I was interested only in fulfilling my mission. But I decided to lend my talents to the opposition. There were several reasons for this. For one thing, since my purpose was to change things in our society, it seemed to me I would have more scope to point out deficiencies from the opposition benches. After all, I didn't want power – I wanted my philosophy to be heard. For another thing, the opposition members were mostly East Indian and my name – I had it changed back to Parmanandansingh – would give me an advantage over the other candidates. And it seemed to me that the Government was at that time extremely unpopular, especially with the important voting bloc of the jamettes, and I would be surer to win my seat in the opposition constituency.

Nonetheless, when the day for my screening came, I was quite nervous. The interview was held at my home, which is to say my father's home. He had retired now and spent his days eating mango chow and watching *The Young and the Restless*. My stepmother spent the day cooking, washing and ensuring my father did not dribble. With a twinge of longing for what might have been, I wondered if I would ever have so perfect a marriage in my twilight years. My father didn't even notice when I came back home. It was a contented life.

I had made all the preparations I could think to ensure the interview went as smoothly as possible. There were cold beers in the refrigerator, and I had put out a bottle of rum and glasses in the living-room.

I do not think I need go into great detail on the campaign which eventually won me a seat in the House of Representatives, as our parliament is mysteriously called.

I took to politics like a fish to water. There were two other candidates running against me – one from the ruling party, one independent – and in my very first campaign speech I told the crowd that I had met the government candidate, that he had told me he expected to be defeated and that the independent had promised to vote for me.

Unfortunately, I had not realized the media were attending that meeting, and the next day my jocular comments were published in the newspapers.

Both candidates immediately issued categorical denials, the government candidate even going so far to say that I was a former Information Ministry official and had been fired because of inaccuracies and an outright penchant for lying.

I recovered nicely, though, saying that even if they hadn't told me so in words, their body language had registered defeat. Moreover, contrary to reports, I said I had actually been fired from the ministry because of accuracy.

However, the deputy leader did call me up and advise me that, while the public didn't expect truth, they did want a semblance of it.

'You can't insult the voters' intelligence,' he said, 'because they don't have much. But you can't treat them like the fools they are, either.'

Obviously, he didn't know that I had by this time of life acquired the habit of recording all telephone conversations, as well as personal ones, or he might not have been so frank. Nonetheless, it was an important political precept which I never forgot and, since then, I have always tried to treat the masses as though they have a little intelligence. Anything above that, and the crowd tends to get bored and pelt the platform with tomatoes and, occasionally, rotten eggs. And, as this brought back painful memories of Gloria, I resisted any temptation to discuss issues,

146

but concentrated on the moral, intellectual and physical deficiencies of my opponents. The last category, especially, enjoyed marked success. The candidate for the ruling party was quite overweight and I described him as 'having enough chins to open his own bakery'. The independent candidate, I said, 'had a nose sharp enough to slice the bread the other one baked, and spread butter, too'. Even if I say so myself, it went over well with the crowd.

But, sparkling oratory or not, the result was a foregone conclusion. Besides the clear unpopularity of the government, besides the fact that the constituency was mostly East Indian and voting in Trinidad was always along ethnic lines, I had God on my side.

As the history books record, I won with a 52 per cent margin and, on 4 May, proudly took my seat in parliament. A well-padded one with arms and an adjustable backrest. You could sleep quite comfortably in it when the Friday evening session got tedious.

Chapter Nine

There will be time, there will be time
To prepare a face to meet the faces that you meet.

From 'The Love Song of J. Alfred
Prufrock' by T.S. Eliot

It was not too long before I made my presence felt in the House. Attending to constituency matters proved a relatively easy task for a man of my experience and ability. I went to my office religiously once a week, staying there the entire three hours. While there, I conscientiously listened to complaints and requests for assistance from constituents, and promised to do what I could. For those who were persistent, I reminded them that I was merely an opposition MP. Many of my colleagues, I should mention, did not do half as much.

As a representative of the people, and bearing in mind my deeper purpose, I concentrated my energies on parliament. Every week I harassed the political leader, Mr Maharaj, and Chief Whip Savita Sackal, to let me speak. Eventually, my persistence paid off. They saw how committed I was and agreed to let me raise an Urgent Matter of Public Importance.

'Just get off my back,' Mr Maharaj said jokingly.

For readers who may not be familiar with parliamentary procedure, let me offer a brief word of explanation. Every week, an MP raised an issue which he considered urgent enough to discuss in place of whatever was previously scheduled to be discussed in the House. This was called an 'Urgent Matter of Public Importance' and was usually brought up by the opposition members since government MPs seemed quite content to discuss only legislation. The Speaker of the House would listen to the member's application and decide if it was indeed so urgent an issue as to warrant discussion in the House. And the very week the political leader gave me leave to raise an issue, I had received a very serious complaint from one of my constituents.

So, on 29 August at 1.57 p.m., I gave my maiden speech in parliament. I wore a beige suit with a peach-coloured shirt, dark green tie, powder-blue socks and brown leather shoes. I also purchased a videotape of the session from one of the television stations later. Copies with a written script giving an insight into my thoughts at the time are available to readers at a reasonable price. (Fifty per cent discount on video with the purchase of this book.) The event went as follows.

The moment the Speaker asked if there was any urgent matter of public importance, I leaped at once to my feet.

'The Chair recognizes the Honourable Member for – ' says the Speaker.

I wait, wondering whom he is referring to.

'Mr Parmanandansingh,' the Speaker prompts.

I give a visible start of surprise. (I had never been called 'Honourable' before and so was a little confused.)

'Yes, Mr Speaker,' I say, my faultless accent reverberating throughout the high-ceilinged chamber. 'I wish to draw your attention to a public matter of urgent importance or, rather, the other way around.'

'Yes, Mr Parmanandansingh,' says the Speaker who, I notice, has a nervous twitch around the mouth.

'Recently, a garbage dump was opened in my constituency. Now I have no objection to the disposal of garbage *per se*. In fact, I consider it as a necessary social service as, I am sure, do all my honourable colleagues on both sides of this august House, even in other months. But, Mr Speaker, this garbage dump has begun

149

attracting corbeaux to my constituency. The corbeau, Mr Speaker, is a scavenging bird . . .'

'I am well aware of what a corbeau is, Mr Parmanandansingh,' the Speaker interrupts. 'Could you get to the point?'

I am not slow on the uptake (unless jokes are being told or when reading modern poetry), but I begin to suspect that the Speaker is prejudiced. This is to be confirmed just a few moments later.

'Well, Mr Speaker, as you might also know, my constituency is a rural one and the presence of the corbeaux has affected the farmers in my area. One of my constituents has reported the loss of seven chickens, 12 ducks and three pigs. Yet another has lost eight chickens, two ducks and 13 pigeons. But, Mr Speaker, that is not the worst of it.'

The Speaker's nervous twitch prevents him speaking for a few moments. I wonder briefly why parliament had chosen a man so afflicted for this important position.

'It isn't?' he says finally.

'No, it isn't!' I shout, banging my hand on the table.

There is a brief pause while the clerk sponges up the water spilled from my glass because of my passionate gesture. I am quite certain the look the woman gives me is a dirty look, and I wonder if she is suitable for the important post she holds.

And then I see it! The woman has a twitch just like the Speaker's – clearly a family trait – and I gain my first inkling of how rife nepotism is in government.

Nonetheless, I bravely continue. I have never been a man to be easily intimidated, unless hairy spiders are involved.

'No, Mr Speaker, that is *not* the worst of it. Another constituent reported that when she went out in her backyard, she found her three-year-old son actually being attacked by one of these corbeaux. The child could have been carried off, Mr Speaker, and I think we need to urgently discuss the important matter of proper garbage disposal in this country.'

There are, of course, protestations from the government benches and even mocking laughter. The Speaker rises to his feet.

'I have decided that this does not qualify as an urgent matter of public importance. We shall move on to the first bill.'

The Speaker gasps a little as he speaks – guiltily, I think. Needless to say, I am totally shocked. 'But, Mr Speaker, people's lives are in danger . . .!' I protest.

'I have ruled,' says the Speaker, and sits down.

'But,' I begin, for I am as tenacious as a bulldog, and a man of iron will besides. But my own chief whip, Miss Sackal, tells me to sit down!

It was then that I truly understood the many obstacles I was to face in the nation's parliament. Miss Sackal was a woman of strong personality, though. I wondered how she would look in leather. And so ended my maiden parliamentary speech.

Nonetheless, despite the many barriers, I was resolved to do my best. Having struggled for so long and reached so far, I was not about to be stymied. Having raised an urgent matter of public importance, I was now intent on making a significant contribution to legislation which came to the House. Laws, I realized, were extremely important. It was law which determined how people behaved. In fact, I thought that if I weren't an MP, I would have been a lawyer. It was better to be an MP, of course, since you actually approved the laws. And, of course, you didn't have to wear black robes and a powdered wig – a not insignificant advantage. In parliament, MPs wore suits only, but the Speaker did wear a robe and a powdered wig. Since I wore only a suit and a toupée, I considered myself, as an MP, significantly better off.

For a long time, however, I had no chance to make any contribution to the laws of the land. I bided my time, understanding that my inexperience would work against me, but time was on my side. After all, after I had been in the House for a while, I would soon be able to claim my rights as a long-sitting member. It was the system and I had to work within it. I attended parliament every Friday without fail, and there I observed carefully, learned well and took some well-deserved naps.

After a few months, on 7 December at 2.10 p.m., I made my first parliamentary contribution to the laws of the country. The legislation was an addendum to the Telephone Act, which sought to facilitate the setting up of a new electronic system. In truth, I was quite surprised that Mr Sant asked me to deal with it in the debate. It was an apparently innocuous piece of legislation but, the minute I looked at it, I saw the threat it posed to our society.

I told Mr Sant nothing of this. I was by this time an old hand at the politics game, and I knew, in order to be successful, one had to keep one's hand close to one's chest. The political leader and the other MPs, it was clear to me, had missed the deeper implications of this bill, or else they would have hogged the debate for themselves. This, I knew, was my big chance. Not only would I be defending my country from a pernicious influence, but I would also be showing my colleagues on both sides of the House the rapier sharpness of my mind.

The new system this bill introduced in the Telephone Act necessitated the introduction of new instruments with push-button dials. Unlike our present handsets, these push-button dials, imported from the United States, had three letters to go with each number. And therein lay the trap which no one had seen, though I am sure the government was well aware of it and had expected to slip it past the opposition. But they had not reckoned on the presence of Paras Parmanandansingh. (Videotapes and scripts also available as above.)

On that auspicious day, after the communications minister had introduced the bill, I caught the eye of the Speaker, who acknowledged me. With, I admit, some butterflies in my stomach, I rose to my feet.

Now in parliament, I should explain, all members are required to conduct themselves as though the members from the other side do not exist. Which is to say, even when we are replying to remarks made by members on the other side, we must address our remarks to the Speaker. This prevents the debate from descending into vulgar abuse, though the sitting members throw a lot of slanderous remarks. However, since they are sitting, it is as though they have not spoken.

'Mr Speaker,' I say, looking fixedly at the communications minister, 'the Honourable Minister tells us that the government wishes to introduce updated communications technology to Trinidad in order to improve communication. If this is all they wished to do, I would have no objection. But, Mr Speaker, this is clearly a government which takes no cognizance of its deeper social responsibilities.

'I have no objection to improved communications *per se*. Indeed, I often use the telephone to discuss business or make dates with my women friends, sometimes at the same time . . .'

At this point, the Speaker interrupts me to ask if this is relevant. Clear prejudice.

'Very much so, Mr Speaker,' I say. I was not at all intimidated, for there were no hairy spiders in evidence. 'I mention the fact to show that I have a healthy understanding of the uses of the telephone. In fact, having examined the present bill in some detail, I might even go so far as to say that I understand the uses of the telephone better than many persons. Perhaps even better than the Honourable Minister . . .'

The minister rises immediately to his feet and I sit down.

'A point of order, Mr Speaker,' he says. 'As communications minister, I have made a thorough study of the country's telephone system. I have access to information which my Honourable colleague does not. I therefore resent the Honourable Member's implication that I am not as *au courant* with the telephone as I ought to be.'

'I bow to the Honourable Minister's superior knowledge,' I say at once, never too proud to yield a point. The Speaker, once again afflicted by that strange twitch, nods at me to continue.

'However,' I say, 'that still does not alter the fact that there are

153

aspects of this legislation which are entirely pernicious and which can contribute to the further moral breakdown of our society!'

There is a murmur in the House at my assertion, and several members wake up. The Speaker looks at me intently.

I continue, 'In the United States of America, a far more lax and permissive society than our own, it is well known that this system is used to make words out of telephone numbers. One understands the reason for this. Because of the size of that country, telephone numbers consist of as many as ten digits. By matching letters to numbers, it becomes easier to remember telephone codes. But in Trinidad,' here I pause dramatically, 'we use only seven digits, and three of those are standard codes! Why, then, should the govern- ment be so insistent on this country having a system which it clearly does not need? Are the Honourable Members on the other side trying to imply that the ordinary citizens of this country, who certainly have enough intelligence to use a telephone, are unable to remember their telephone numbers? Or perhaps – reluctant though I am to suggest such a thing – unable to write them down?'

The communications minister gets to his feet. And it is then I notice the awful, unbelievable thing. His lips are also twitching! I know then that, no matter how well I speak, the Speaker will obviously favour the minister who, it seems, is also a relative. Nonetheless, I take my seat calmly.

'Mr Speaker,' says the minister, looking as innocent as though he wasn't speaking even to a distant cousin, 'I wish to assure the Honourable Member that the government has no such intention. We have every confidence in the intelligence of the citizenry at large, though I am not so sanguine about some of their representatives.'

Something – I cannot tell what – causes a titter of laughter in the House at this point. But I get to my feet with a heavy heart and, although I now know more than ever that the deck is stacked against me, I continue bravely. Whatever my other deficiencies, I have never lacked raw courage.

'I am willing to give the Honourable Minister the benefit of the doubt,' I say and, despite my gloom, I cheer up a little at my happy phrasing. 'However, if the government is not malicious, then it is at the very least careless. I am not certain which is the greater evil.'

'Come, come, Mr Parmanandansingh,' says the Speaker, displaying his family twitch for the entire House to see. 'Surely your language is a little strong.'

Well, I was not about to bow to such obvious partisanship.

'A bill with such pernicious provisions deserves strong language, Mr Speaker,' I say, speaking, I am afraid, quite firmly.

The Speaker leans forward.

'How so?' he asks, and I must admit that, despite his favouritism, he seems genuinely fascinated.

'A simple mathematical equation, Mr Speaker,' I reply and, even knowing I am fighting a losing battle, the Joy of Correctness sustains me in that moment. 'Our telephones have seven digits. Three are in code, and therefore will not require letters. Instead the letters will, in all probability, be applied to the remaining letters to form a word. Three from seven leaves four. Therefore, we will have a telephone system which has . . .' I pause . . . 'four-letter words.'

There is blank silence in the House while the members, whose brains are not as quick or as deep as my own, seek to grasp this concept.

'Four-letter words!' I continue. 'In houses where there might even be small children . . .!'

I was getting into my stride and, even now, I think I might have waxed so eloquent I could even have persuaded the Speaker to suspend his family loyalties.

But there is a sudden interruption at this point – again I do not see what caused it – as the entire House erupts into roars of laughter. The government benches are virtually shrieking, my own colleagues are hooting. Even the Speaker is twisting helplessly in his chair. Maybe somebody had broken wind in the public gallery. The videotape gives no clue.

I do not smile, but stand waiting. I think the issue – technology once again threatening to undermine morality – too serious to warrant such an interruption. In fairness to my colleagues, however, I acknowledge that it is difficult not to laugh when, as I assume has happened, someone passes wind audibly.

When, after some minutes, the mirth subsides, the Speaker says, 'I hope the Honourable Member will forgive us our lapse.'

He wipes some tears from his eyes, and I am genuinely moved at his regret. And then, just as I am about to resume, my own leader pulls the carpet out from under me. Metaphorically speaking, that is.

'Perhaps, Mr Speaker,' says Mr Maharaj, getting to his feet, quite improperly, 'we might have an early tea-break today.'

I sit down, not because I am following proper procedure, but because I am so shocked my legs can no longer support me.

'An excellent idea, Mr Maharaj,' says the Speaker, and the sitting is suspended. And so ended my first parliamentary debate.

I was so angry, I left the building at once and went home without even speaking to anyone. It was a terrible end to my first contribution, but it made me all the more determined to make my presence felt in public life. In retrospect, I may have seemed naïve, given the forces pitted against me. Even my own political leader was undermining me. Later, I once overheard him say, 'Paras is the kind of man who's so well-informed he thinks ethnic cleansing is a new kind of detergent.' In fact, I have never even heard of this brand but, as I was to learn, it was *because* Mr Maharaj considered me so well-informed that he foiled me at every turn. However, it is the man who refuses to acknowledge the odds who attains success or loses his entire life's savings at poker. I remember that day I went home and wrote a short, rousing poem to encourage myself.

> Give me a pen, a beer and a fight
> And on my lips a song!

And I will to death defend my right
Even if I'm wrong!

Later, when I assumed the role of Paras P., this became, as it were, my martial hymn. It aptly expressed, in my opinion, my devil-may-care spirit, my basic values and even my occasional self-doubt.

Despite the unsatisfactory outcome of my maiden speech, I had at least got my foot in the door. Nor did I have any intention of now resting on my laurels. The amendments to the Telephone Act were duly passed, but I knew a defeat in one battle did not mean I had lost the war.

But, sure enough, it was not long after this that further legislation was introduced by the communications minister to facilitate satellite television and even cable. When I saw what was on some of these channels, I was appalled. Obscene language and full frontal nudity. Explicit sex scenes. Not a night passed when there was not some movie, show or even documentary guaranteed to corrupt in some form or fashion. Every night there were sex, violence and liberal ideas. My nation was sliding down the slippery slope of moral degeneracy. And it had, of course, begun with the amendments to the Telephone Act.

I was saddened, but not surprised.

I continued keeping a sharp eye on government legislation, looking out for those things I knew my colleagues would miss. They saw only the obvious stratagems of government to gain greater power through legislation – giving more powers to minis-ters in enforcing the law through drug trafficking legislation, public order acts and employment practices. But I – and it often seemed I alone – knew that the real danger would come through seemingly innocuous bills. It was there our real social breakdown would occur. After all, did it really matter if a government minister could directly hire and fire persons to head the police service or the public service? Did it matter if ministers had salary increases approved by parliament? Did it really matter if opposition politicians or trade unionists could be arrested for causing a public disturbance?

No, these were not the real threat. Once right-thinking people behaved Correctly, after all, such legislation made no impact on the society. But what about the bill to introduce air-conditioned buses in the public transport service?

I argued strenuously against this in parliament, pointing out that these buses, which were to run alongside the cheaper, non air-conditioned buses, would have the effect of deepening class divisions in our society. Schoolchildren, I pointed out, who travelled on the air-conditioned buses, would snub their less fortunate classmates who arrived at school perspiring. They might even nickname those who travelled in the non air-conditioned vehicles 'stinker'.

But this bill passed and the buses were introduced. And I feared for my country. It often seemed to me that I was the only MP who saw so deeply, so truly, into society. Others saw only the practical, the surface, the obvious. I saw the human, moral side. I take no credit for this. It was the spirit of God within me.

Despite this, I soon noticed that the political leader was making deliberate efforts to prevent me from speaking in parliament. At first, I could not understand this. Only after much thinking did it occur to me that he was envious! Clearly, my sophisticated speaking manner, and the depth and range of my understanding on a wide variety of topics, had aroused his ire, especially as I was a mere back-bencher. Perhaps he was even afraid I might eventually challenge his leadership of the party. Little did he know that I had no desire to be political leader, though I suppose he did get invited to all the best cocktail parties.

Even so, I was in a quandary. I had attained a position of influence to be sure, and you could often catch my visage on the *Parliamentary Report* on television. This may have been enough for some men, but not for me. And now I was being prevented from fulfilling my larger purpose. My constituency work, and my face on the TV, could inspire only so many people. I considered resigning, but what purpose would that have served except relieving me of a very useful salary? I even considered joining the government side. But, although I was sure the government would welcome such a gifted speaker as myself, that was also the reason I might, ironically, *not* be welcomed. After all, I had given them many telling blows, using elegant language. I had revealed much of their irresponsibility, nefariousness and nefarious irresponsibility.

And even as I struggled with this complex problem, an issue arose which was to lead to what I call my 'Crisis of Conscience'. At the time, it seemed to me that God was really putting too much on my plate, though I admit I had always tried to serve Him well. But when the confidential report, written so many years ago when I was an information officer, on 'The incidence of blood loss in citizens' surfaced in parliament in the hands of the opposition, I truly felt God was trying me too high. 'My God, my God, why have you forsaken me?' I remember praying.

But I should have known that, as always, He had a Plan.

Chapter Ten

We entertain Him always like a stranger,
And, as at first, still lodge Him in the manger.

Anonymous (16th century)

The appearance of this report naturally caused a great furore, not only in parliament, but in the entire country. The political leader produced it quite unexpectedly one afternoon during a debate on, of all things, public accountability. But Mr Maharaj, among his myriad faults, has always had bad timing.

Indeed, I remember clearly an incident where, meeting him just before the Friday session began, I told him I would like to see him to discuss my next contribution to the House. He said (and naturally I have this on tape), 'Check me around six at my office.'

When I arrived at six o' clock precisely, Mr Maharaj was not there and his secretary had no messages, save in her eyes. (I often had this effect on women, especially since becoming a man of influence.) After I had waited for two hours, it dawned on me that he was not coming. And when I met him the following week, he said, 'Sorry, had a previous engagement.' And I have that recorded, too.

Now if a political leader cannot manage his time better than that, what hope is there for our country? MPs are always being invited out to various social occasions, and political leaders more so. When I consider, with his careless time management, how many embarrassed hosts Mr Maharaj must have left strewn, like broken crockery, over the passage of years, to say nothing of the numerous disappointed guests strewn, if I may extend my metaphor, over the dining-room of weeks, it is no wonder the man never became prime minister. What hope can there be for any politician, or indeed a leader in any sphere, who does not attend as many cocktail parties as he can? Some might argue that we demand too much of our leaders, and to a certain extent this is true, but there is always a price to pay for power.

But I digress.

By producing the report in the midst of a debate on accountability, the political leader not only caught the government off-guard, but also confused them thoroughly since they weren't sure if the health minister or the finance minister should respond. And, while the ministers checked hurriedly through the Standing Orders, Mr Maharaj was able to read through most of the report, including the comments written – officially – by the commissioner on how best to ensure the issue never became a public scandal. Little did I know when I wrote those words that my eloquence would return to haunt me. But worse was to come.

'And I fully intend,' said Mr Maharaj at the conclusion of his speech, 'to leak this report to the media.'

It was Mr Maharaj's use of the word 'leak' which brought to me a startling revelation. Despite his bad record of attendance at key cocktail parties and not a few free dinners, Mr Maharaj had proved to be an able politician. And I knew that, while government politics often take place at black-tie affairs (though some ministers prefer to be bound with red silk scarves by their mistresses), opposition politics, like weekly journalism, depends heavily on what is overheard in restrooms. Indeed, I have known some of my more dedicated colleagues to spend hours in the toilet just to get inside information, though this cost them a small fortune in Mexican food.

Little did I realize then how important a role this revelation was to play in my own future.

161

But the fact he was giving the report to the media occasioned me considerable concern. It was not beyond the bounds of possibility, I felt, that an alert editor might notice the similarity in writing style between the author of that report and my own. It was true that I had not remained long in journalism, but my prose was, of course, distinctive. The editors would not have forgotten me.

That some people at the Information Ministry might remember it was I who had originally penned the report worried me not at all. Even if anyone did, it was unlikely they would tell anyone. Refusing to give out information at government ministries was *de rigueur* and at the Information Ministry such reluctance was naturally developed *par excellence*. Pardon my French.

No, my real concern was the media. If this connection came out, I would naturally be drummed out of the party at once. I decided, therefore, to 'take in front before in front took me', as the local phrase goes. What was needed was a counter-measure, a distraction. The issue of efficiency in the public service came up, and I spoke against it. But the matter died a natural death, since everyone realized an efficient public service was an impossible dream.

I then attempted, as a matter of urgent public importance, to raise the emotive issue of whether dogs in the country were getting the best quality dog food or whether brands which had been rejected in developed countries were being dumped in Third World nations like our own. The motion was rejected by the Speaker, as I had expected, and the political leader gave me a sharp look since I had not informed him of my intention to raise this issue. But what surprised me was that there was not an immediate outcry by animal lovers throughout the length and breadth of the land to have this matter debated. Instead, the issue of government corruption remained on the front burner in the public mind.

So I was back to square one. And I realized I would have to take more direct action if I was to protect myself. Even as the report continued to be debated in parliament, in offices, in rum shops, and in restrooms throughout the land, the conviction grew upon me that it would be only a matter of time before my name was linked to the report. Even those guiding texts of public life – *Jimmy Swaggart on Avoiding Dehydration*, *The Bakkers: Many Comings* and *The Don'ts and Don'ts of Dan Quayle* – proved useless in my hour of need. And then, as I lay in bed thinking hard one night, the answer came to me. I immediately threw away the tissue paper and put the cover back on the jar of Vaseline and sat down to work out my plan.

Since, as I then thought, I could not stop the truth from coming out, what I needed to do was make myself so impervious that even if that happened, my reputation would be inviolable enough to protect me. And what better way to do that than by personally taking up the cause of public accountability! It was an inspired idea, and one I do not think I could have thought of by myself. Clearly I was being guided by a Higher Power.

I applied considerable thought as to the most effective way to go about this task. Co-opting the media would be essential, and here my experience in journalism and sewing proved useful.

I knew it was no use relying on my considerable public speaking abilities to get the kind of attention I wanted. The media hardly ever reported what I said in parliament, no doubt because they considered it too detrimental to the stability of government. So I resolved to go to the other extreme, and not speak at all. The spectacle of a politician refusing to speak would, I felt, be sufficiently unusual to bring the journalists flocking like a bee to honey. But if I were not speaking, how would I get the attention of the public?

The answer, as every great leader throughout history knew, was to make a public spectacle of myself. Jesus Christ did it in the temple, Hitler had his moustache and Gandhi wore a dhoti.

But appearance was also crucial. As a former journalist, I knew nothing grabs attention more readily than a good photograph. And, as a former churchgoer, I knew nothing gave a man a greater appearance of authority than a long, flowing gown. I called up

Choo Choo Chu, who readily agreed to design a statement-making robe for me. When I received his design, I sat down and sewed it myself.

I used white cotton. White represented purity of spirit, a clean character and looked good on film. The material was natural, had been worn by religious men throughout the ages and kept you cool. (Nothing ruins a public image more quickly than sweating. In fact, I have often theorized that this is the real reason so few great leaders are found in the Caribbean or Africa. Nelson Mandela, one might note in this context, seems never to perspire.)

Finally – and this was most difficult of all – I resolved to fast. A silent politician might be interesting for a day, perhaps even two. But a fasting one would show true seriousness of purpose, could become a figure of national interest and might therefore stay in the media's eye for an entire week, if only to make sure he wasn't sneaking in some chocolate cake on the side. Fasting would also demonstrate my spiritual nature, so that if ever it was discovered I was the author of that report, I could say, 'Yes, but I have been without food and cannot be held responsible.' I would become, I hoped, more than a politician to the nation.

And so, with all preparations in place, it remained only to choose my venue. The choice, of course, was obvious. I was protesting against the lack of public accountability and, by implication, corruption in government.

So, wearing my white robe and a holy expression, I began my silent fast on 10 February on the steps of the Finance Ministry. It had been a bit difficult getting the holy expression just right, but after several days studying videotapes of Jimmy Swaggart, Sai Baba and several live goldfish, I had the technique down to an exact science.

I had sent an anonymous note to all the media houses informing them that a well-known MP would be sitting on the steps of the Finance Ministry that day. I had included a description of what I was wearing and mentioned that Choo Choo was the designer, not only to whet their appetites, but just in case anyone else was sitting on the Finance Ministry steps that morning. (It is this care in anticipating every eventuality which has brought me to the position I am in today. I would, I think, have made a good general.)

However, it turned out that I was the only one protesting that morning. The photographers and reporters duly arrived. The photographers took pictures and the reporters attempted to ask me some questions, such as what house I worked for and what my name was. I thought that, as political reporters, they should have known these things already. So I merely shook my head silently and looked holy.

That first day was very difficult. The sun was hot and people kept tripping over me. However, a few persons did put money in my hand. I allowed myself to drink water. But this made me want to urinate and, though there was nothing in the rules against it, I did not think I should go to the toilet. So I sat and suffered, drawing strength from the thought that crucifixion must have been worse. (Though it couldn't have been *much* worse.)

And it was then that the great inspiration came to me! I had been following the example of great leaders throughout history in order to make my point. But, in modern times, one needed an additional advantage. And that was a catchy name! The reporter had even asked what name I was using, but I had not understood what she was getting at.

At that time, the fashion was to use a letter after your name. I thought of Paras X, but it sounded too much like a scientific experiment and that letter had been used already – once by Malcolm and, in Trinidad itself, by Michael. The letter T was also taken and, besides, I didn't own that many gold chains.

Then I thought of using Paras Parmanandansingh PhD but, although it was alliterative, I thought misunderstandings might arise. Besides, the thing had to be short and pithy.

And that was when it hit me! The *mot juste*: 'Paras P.' It was philosophically, auditorily, semantically and spellingly perfect. After all, was I not here because of a leak? Did not urine represent the eternal cycle? Water, the first element, went into man and

165

came out again with his elements – the divine and mortal in one. Yet there was humility in it, for are we not all part of the nitrogen cycle? Do we not all return to the clay from which we came? There was also the inspired implication that, instead of being an 'MP', which was the kind of person T.S. Eliot was talking about in his poem about hollow men, I was a 'Full P' or a man of substance. Language is a powerful tool, and human beings are deeply influenced by such subtleties, though I will admit they are usually influenced by more obvious factors, like women with large breasts in low-cut blouses. Even so, Paras P. was the kind of name which could even be put neatly into a headline. All in all, I felt it was a letter you couldn't go wrong with.

Realizing too late that I should have taken care of this important detail before beginning my protest, I was not too surprised that there was almost nothing about me in the papers the following day. In fact, one paper had gotten completely the wrong angle and carried a photograph of me on its inside pages with a short article headlined 'Mute male models'.

Still, the day hadn't been a complete loss. I had come up with my new name and made seven dollars and 43 cents from people who were either contributing to my cause or thought I was begging. (I was not sure which.)

But I realized that I would have to communicate in some form or fashion with the media. Yet I had taken a vow not to speak. It was a difficult situation. This time, the note I sent off – which I probably should have sent in the first place – mentioned that leader Paras P., an opposition member of parliament, would be protesting the lack of government accountability on the steps of the Finance Ministry. It was a very precise note. When the reporters actually came, I was planning to communicate without writing. I could not risk expressing myself too much on paper in case some alert newshound linked my style to the report.

As I expected, the reporters began clustering around as soon as I arrived and took up my post on the concrete steps. At first, I remained silent, pointing to my mouth and making a motion as

166

though zipping my fly to indicate I would not speak or eat. But then, as they persisted in the desperate way reporters have, I relented and took out the hand puppets I had brought along in case of such a contingency. It was made more difficult by the fact that my left hand was sore and so I tended to stutter.

The first interview, stumbling but hesitant, went as follows.

'Who are you?'

This question, obviously from a reporter who had not troubled to read my note, upset me not a little. For a second I thought, as V.S. Naipaul would have done, of biting him in the leg. But further reflection convinced me that this would not help my cause. Besides, the question gave me a chance to introduce my new name.

'I am Paras P.'

Misunderstanding my signs, they stood aside courteously to let me go to the ornamental plants, but I eventually got them to understand my true meaning.

'Why are you sitting on the steps of the Finance Ministry?'

'Because I am fed up, like all right-thinking citizens, with the lack of public accountability in this nation.'

'Do you think this gesture will have any effect?'

'If it leads to the hiring of just one more accountant, I will have done my duty.'

'What would you like to see done about corruption?'

'As a nation, we need to be more spiritual. That is part of the message I am trying to get across here.'

'How so?'

'I am a holy man.'

'But didn't you say you were a politician?' one reporter asked, with the happy air of having caught me in a contradiction.

It was then I took the biggest gamble of my life. I reached up – and removed my hair-piece.

'No longer.'

The reporters gasped. And well they might have, for no politician in the history of Trinidad had ever resigned from office or admitted he wore a toupée. I also figured that those who saw me

167

with my true headline would never connect me to the full-haired person who had written the report. It is not given to every man to leave his younger self behind him so easily. Indeed, I have known some men, trying to retain their youthful image, go so far as to put on an earring and grow a pony-tail so they can look like teenage girls.

At this stage in the interview, the questions grew more penetrating and controversial.

'Are the steps to the Finance Ministry well swept?' the same reporter who had asked my name queried. He was obviously from a weekly paper.

'No. I shall have to wash my robe tonight, which is a Choo Choo Chu original.'

By this time, my hands were getting tired. I was not used to talking so much. So, reluctantly, the interview was concluded.

The next day, both daily papers and a weekly carried front-page pictures of me in full colour sitting on the steps of the Finance Ministry. The headlines in the dailies read 'Fast for corruption' and 'Silence on accountability'. The weekly paper's headline said, 'Finance Ministry can't afford brooms'.

I had become a national figure and, for the first time in weeks, did not worry about the report and my connection to it. I was beyond such petty things now.

Several crucial events occurred during the next two weeks to shape the course of my future. Reporters interviewed me daily to get my views on politics, the economy, the education system, religion, marriage, the latest Test match, vegetarian diets, the new spring fashions and many more important issues of local and international interest. I had become a guru of the national psyche, and my only regret was that I had not tried to grow a beard. But, in everything I said, I extolled the virtues of Correctness.

The government, of course, could not afford to ignore the issues I was raising. In fact, that very week the finance minister, who had hitherto completely ignored my contributions in parliament, issued a release to the press stating categorically that the Finance Ministry's steps were swept daily by a cadre of trained and committed sweepers. In fact, for the rest of my stay the steps were indeed spotless. I realized my campaign was having an effect.

The political leader also came to see me – the first time, I believe, he had actually sought my company.

'So I hear you resign?' he said.

I nodded.

'Well, we will have to hold a by-election.'

I nodded.

'You won't be running?'

I shook my head. He smiled and held out his hand.

'Well, good luck,' he said. 'Make sure and vote for us.'

Mr Maharaj turned and left. I admired his iron self-control, for the disappointment he must have felt at losing me, particularly now I had become a national icon, must have been acute.

Meanwhile, my protest gained support throughout the length and breadth of the country. At first, only the people I had hired came and sat with me or fetched me lunch. (I lost two pounds in the first two days and figured, for medical reasons, I should resume my normal diet. After all, I could not serve my people effectively if I was faint from malnutrition.) But it was not long before people I had never even spoken to or laid eyes on were smiling at me or saying hello. One or two even came and sat with me for a while and we would converse about Life and other philosophical matters. (I had also decided to talk, since conversing with hand puppets often led to misinterpretations of my message. Christ, I believe, had the same problem with his parables.)

'The sun real hot today,' one companion would suggest.

'Indeed. But what is heat but the perception of our skin? And is not Beauty only skin deep, and Truth not Beauty? This is Correctness.'

These aphorisms came easily out of me. I felt I had tapped into a fountain of Divine Wisdom. And, though I did not ask, several people gave me money.

'So how you going?' another would ask in passing.

'All progress is illusory, and perfection lies in being still in the Godhead. This is how to attain Correctness!' I would shout back, resolved to impart wisdom even to the casual passerby. A lesser guru would have been content with a 'I going good'.

For the two weeks that I sat on the steps of the Finance Ministry, I must have gathered several hundred loyal followers, for I never saw the same faces twice.

Yet, despite these thousands of persons to whom I spread my message of Correctness even in those early days, there was one who stood out above all others: Devika Lakshmi Singh, who was to become my wife.

She first appeared to me as a pair of slim legs clad in white stockings. I looked up to see a high forehead and dark, burning eyes.

'How can I help you, sister?' I asked in the gentle voice with which God had now favoured me.

'I want to have your child,' she said in a deep, intense voice.

I understood her at once and clasped her hand gently. Our sweats mingled like holy water.

'Sit, sister, sit and let us talk awhile.'

Devika, it turned out, had a direct relationship with God. Many times, she told me, she had spoken to angels sent by Him and seen His face plastered across the sky when she prayed. She told me how once, walking down the stairs in her building, she tripped *and did not fall*! It could only have been divine intervention.

Naturally, when she read of me and my mission in the newspaper, she realized at once that I also was specially chosen. And, she admitted to me shyly, she liked my bald head and had just received a small inheritance. I realized at once that this was my preordained mate. It was, I knew in my deepest soul, Correct that we should be together.

We were married within two weeks.

170

In truth, Devika came along at just the correct time, for interest in my protest was already on the wane. I had done all I could on this particular issue, and the attention span of the general public never lasts very long. When the reporters started asking my opinion of the latest situation on *The Young and the Restless*, and then stopped coming entirely, I knew it was time to quit.

But God had other plans for me. I was beginning to see a pattern here.

Chapter Eleven

The cold whip-adder unespied
With waved passes there shall glide
Too near thee, and thou must abide
The ringed blindworm hard beside.

From 'The cold whip-adder' by
Gerard Manley Hopkins

Despite the obvious diminishing of media interest, it was no easy decision to abandon my arduous task of sitting on the steps of the Finance Ministry. I had virtually become a fixture there, like a lamp-post. In fact, several times I had had to drive away stray dogs.

But I had, as I say, done all I could and people weren't contributing funds to my cause as readily as before. It is the kind of world we live in today – fast-paced, lacking commitment, always seeking new thrills.

I had established my reputation, but what I needed was a new cause. Something worthwhile, uplifting and financially renumerative.

I had by this time moved into my wife's house. Her inheritance, wisely invested, provided a small but steady income. My father had died and left me land. I had rented out the family home, persuading my stepmother she would be much happier in one of the many excellent establishments for the aged. My father had left no will and when she called me a 'sly little pothound', as reported in a story in a weekly newspaper, I am sure she was misquoted.

The journalistic profession had, sadly, gone rapidly downhill in the years since I had left it.

At any rate, although we were able to afford food, a car, an apartment near the city, regular cocktail parties and the occasional shopping trip to Caracas, Devika and I were living a desperate existence. Had I been single and without purpose I would have withstood the rigours, for mine is a hardy character. But I could not bear to see my wife pining away because she could not afford those trifles without which a woman is not truly a woman. When I tell you that a $400 dress and a gold Rolex were beyond our means, you will understand the hand-to-mouth existence we led in those impecunious days. And, more importantly still, I needed money to spread my philosophy of Correctness.

Then God, whom I have always viewed as my Cosmic Banker, stepped in.

Ten years ago, there was a government minister who was accused of accepting a substantial sum of money and, what is worse, a blonde prostitute from an American corporation which had won a lucrative building contract from the government. The matter had been investigated by the government and closed. But now the same corporation had been investigated by the US authorities on another matter, and uncovered evidence that the minister had indeed taken money and a blonde prostitute.

Thus, another furore about government accountability flared up mere months after the first one had subsided. My old friend, Dr Maron Dopak, a man who was always concerned about integrity in public life, commented, 'The most shocking aspect of the entire issue is that a government minister, as a black man given power since colonialism ended, should be offered a blonde prostitute by this American corporation. Could he not at least have paid for her services out of his bribe?'

Now that the affair had come to light, the government had no choice but to sue the American corporation for breach of contract and depriving local girls of a minister's custom. The corporation had argued that it was merely following the normal business practice of establishing good relations with a client. It was a good point, and for a time it seemed as though the government had no case.

But then lawyers for the state argued that, by offering said minister a highly paid blonde prostitute, the corporation was using discriminatory employment practices. They even got a spokesman from the National American Association for the Advancement of Colored People. It was then that the corporation decided to settle out of court. The Caribbean has always produced legal luminaries.

In that same week, an American teenager was whipped in Singapore for chewing gum in a public place. The affair got considerable international attention. Surveys were done of countries where whipping was practised and Trinidad was mentioned since, some weeks earlier, an 11-year-old boy was whipped for having cocaine rocks in his possession.

But the reader will want to know how all this affected me.

Well, *Newsweek* sent a reporter to Trinidad to do a story on the scandal. My former sitting stand on the corruption issue came to the attention of the magazine's reporter and he interviewed me and, later, quoted me in his article.

> Paras P., as he calls himself, says, 'Corruption and a general lack of Correct behaviour is what is plaguing my country and, indeed, the world today. I agree with the authorities here and I agree with those in Singapore.'
>
> When asked what he intends to do, Mr P. said, 'Start a Centre for Correctness.'

In fact, when the *Newsweek* reporter posed that question to me, I had no idea what I intended. But the answer, as if it were divinely inspired, simply leapt to my lips.

The more I thought about it, the more feasible the idea seemed. The centre, as I conceived it, would train people from all walks of life in Correct behaviour. And who was better qualified than myself to oversee such training? There would be classes in dinner etiquette, proper pronunciation, answering the telephone, correct dress, proper behaviour when courting and so on. I couldn't do it all myself, of course, but I knew there were scores of old ladies, well trained in these areas, who would be willing to work cheap once they were allowed to display their superior attitudes. This was all these old dears really wanted out of life and I was happy to provide them with the opportunity. And, as the old saying goes, nothing worthwhile is achieved without humiliation.

There would also be classes in writing correctly, an area which I intended to manage myself since I could think of no one better qualified to do so. (Derek Walcott, whom I considered hiring, had, I had heard, a tendency to use four-letter words in his writing and would therefore be inappropriate for this high calling. I had no intention of letting the pernicious effects of the Telephone Act extend to my centre.)

Finally, having discussed all this with Devika, I contacted Magistrate Deborah Blackly-Tolpuddle, who had sentenced the 11-year-old boy to be whipped. There was no one better qualified, I thought, to give advice on Correct legal behaviour. She was very interested in my project and it was she who suggested the idea which was to become the most profitable aspect of the centre – the Whip Shop.

'There is a growing demand for whips locally, as well as internationally,' she pointed out, 'but few places really cater for humans. It seems we place the needs of horses above those of people.'

I agreed it was indeed a topsy-turvy world. And, as I spoke with Magistrate Blackly-Tolpuddle, the Hand of God once again made itself apparent. It turned out she was a direct descendant of a slave once owned by the ancestors of my old friend, Lord Knowsley Rightpaddle Tolpuddle, patron of the Knights of the First Colony.

Indeed, Magistrate Blackly-Tolpuddle proudly traced her ancestry as far back as the hundredth slave owned by Sir Wrightly

'Use the whip and they'll never slip,' I told her.

She was so delighted by this sally that we immediately adopted it for our slogan, along with my martial poem.

Our brochure also points out that the Whip Shop is not only business-oriented. We also have a social conscience. Right now we are trying to organize a programme throughout the nation's schools to establish regular whipping schedules. Keep them in hand in there, we say, and you won't need to keep them in handout here. If we are successful in restoring corporal punishment among youth – and with the crime rate among young people rising, this is a matter which should be given priority before we go out of business – we will supply whips at special educational discount prices.

I might also mention that I test all whips personally, even to the extent of letting Devika tie me up and beat me. This is the real explanation for those photographs published in the weekly newspapers, and I am confident I will win my suit against them. But great men always have their motives misunderstood. I am nothing if not committed to my Mission and, while I certainly do not *enjoy* being tied up and whipped by Devika, I wasn't surprised when our union was blessed.

We also sell blinkers, blindfolds and gags. This is mainly for our Three Monkey Correctness programme, where we train people to hear no evil, speak no evil and see no evil. There is the Diploma programme, which uses soothing music and hypnotism, and the more advanced Degree programme, in which electric shock has proven quite effective. Many of our applicants have shed their dark sides at our centre and contributions, though unrequested, have been quite generous. Much of our earnings are, of course, spent on keeping confidential documents, tapes and video-recordings secure.

I hope eventually to create nothing less than the Perfect Society. Some may say I have an impossible dream, and it is true that I have not found a way to make fried chicken which isn't greasy. But when you are God, or rather when you have God behind you, all things are possible. Even Oprah lost weight. And I am sure my application for Supreme Being will soon be answered.

Meanwhile, all everyone has to do in order to attain perfect happiness and contentment within a well-ordered society is obey my teachings. What could be simpler?

Finis

What if the lines I cast bulge into a book
That has caught nothing?

From Poem XXIX, *Midsummer*
collection, by Derek Walcott

On 19 November, Mr Paras P. suffered a massive stroke. He was rushed to the hospital two days later, when his wife realized what had happened,

'We didn't know anything was wrong,' she explained, sobbing. 'He was watching the Playboy Channel, taking notes for a lecture on moral degeneracy. He told us not to interrupt him. And he wasn't a man who believed in a lot of movement.'

Mr P. never came out of his coma, and passed away quietly on 25 November.

'He died as he would have wished,' said Mrs P. 'Working hard.'

In accordance with Paras P.'s last wishes, Mrs P. intends to preserve the room in which he died exactly as it is, even down to the tissues and Vaseline. In Paras P.'s own words: 'It will be a shrine to guide future generations who may wish to tread the Path of Correctness.'